RUNNING ON EGGS

RUNNING ON EGGS

Anna Levine

FRONT STREET / CRICKET BOOKS

CHICAGO

For my family,
especially Alex, Nimrod, and Tomer

And in memory of my dad

Copyright © 1999 by Anna Levine
All rights reserved
Printed in the United States of America
Designed by John Grandits
Second Printing, 2004

Library of Congress Cataloging-in-Publication Data
Levine, Anna.
    Running on eggs / Anna Levine.
      p.   cm.
    Summary: When Karen and Yasmine become friends as
well as members of a mixed Arab and Jewish track team in
Israel, relatives and friends of both girls disapprove of the
relationship.
    ISBN 0-8126-2875-6
    [1. Jewish-Arab relations Fiction. 2. Track and field
Fiction. 3. Running Fiction. 4. Israel Fiction.] I. Title.
PZ7.L57823Ru 1999
[Fic]—dc21   99-31984

"Do not protect yourself by a fence,
but rather by your friends."

CONTENTS

RUNNING ON EGGS

CHAPTER 1
"YOU WON'T OPEN IT, WILL YOU?"

"Will it blow up?" David asked, his voice barely above a whisper.

"Don't be ridiculous," said Karen.

But she knew she didn't sound convincing and wasn't surprised that David stayed hidden under the table. Karen stared at the faded purple lunchbox sitting on their kitchen counter. Slowly, so as not to jiggle the contents inside, she turned the box around, inspecting it from every angle.

"Five. Four. Three. Two—" David stopped.

Silence.

"One?" His voice squeaked.

"You can come out now, David," said Karen. "It isn't going to explode."

David crawled out cautiously from under his fortress. "What do you think's inside?" he asked.

"Her lunch, probably," said Karen. "Or what's left of it."

"But you won't open it, will you?" David's green eyes grew wider. "It could be a trick to make us *think* it's only a lunchbox, and then when we open it—BOOM!" He slithered down dead to the floor.

"David, stick your tongue back in your mouth—you're drooling. And quit overacting. It's making me nervous."

Lightly tracing the corners of the box with her fingers, Karen hesitated at the plastic clasp. Maybe she wasn't actually supposed to open the lunchbox. The whole situation was frightening, and yet she found herself tingling with excitement. Why me? she wondered. Why did Yasmine choose me?

"How did you say you got it?" asked David, stabbing at the lunchbox with a long wooden spoon.

Karen shoved him away. The box was her responsibility now. She wondered how much she could tell him. He still seemed too young to be trusted with a secret.

"Our lunchboxes look the same," said Karen. "I guess we switched them accidentally."

What she didn't say was how her hand had touched the Arab girl's on the bus ride home from school. Yasmine had tried to make it look like an accident. Tripping by Karen's seat while walking down the bus aisle, Yasmine had dropped her own lunchbox next to Karen's. She paused as if to catch her balance, and they brushed hands. Yasmine's skin had felt warm, almost sweaty. Then, picking up Karen's lunchbox instead of her own, Yasmine had continued to her seat. Karen had no doubt that Yasmine had switched their lunchboxes on purpose.

Sketching over the squiggly Arab writing with her fingertips, Karen tried to sound out the letters.

"What does it say?" asked David, still keeping a safe distance.

"Yasmine, I think."

Karen tried to push away the nagging feeling of guilt. Hadn't she learned anything? Hadn't she been warned? Even kids younger than David would know better, she chided herself. And just that morning in her seventh-grade class she had sat through the same drills that she had gone through since kindergarten:

Be an A student—and survive.

Always Alert An Adult!

Stay away from suspicious objects.

Even innocent-looking packages like lunchboxes could hide explosives. She had seen the news on TV and heard the stories.

The churning feeling in her stomach grew stronger. Yasmine was willing to take a risk, Karen thought to herself. Was she ready, too?

"I still think you're crazy," said David. He grabbed an apple off the table and took a huge bite. "If Mom finds out that you've got a lunchbox that belongs to an Arab, you'll be in *big* trouble."

Karen struggled with her hair band. "Quit trying to scare me. It's no big deal. These Arab kids are our neighbors." She stepped into the bathroom and changed into her track clothes. "I'm going out to train," she said when she came out, and turning to her brother, grabbed him by the shoulder. "Listen here, Mom doesn't have to know about the lunchbox unless you tell on me." She glared at him, making her unspoken threat very clear.

David blinked but didn't budge. "You don't scare me for a second," he said. "And I'm not staying home alone with that box."

"You don't have to," Karen said, grabbing it from the counter. "I'm taking it with me."

David scowled. "Then I'm going with you, too!"

Karen sighed. There was no point in arguing with David. He always got his way. "All right. I'll let you come with me, but only if you tell Mom that you've been out on an undercover mission. Now understand, this time it's like real life, so there's no divulging any secrets, or you'll be demoted from corporal to private in a flash!"

David tipped his baseball cap low over his eyes. "Yes, ma'am!" He puffed out his chest and saluted. "An undercover mission." He glanced timidly at the lunchbox and smiled mischievously. "Maybe we can take one little peek inside before we go?"

Karen shook her head. "No, I don't think we should open it."

David nodded solemnly. "So what are you going to do with it? Bury it? Explode it?"

"Give it back. We're going to meet in the field beyond the avocado grove."

David gulped. "You don't mean no man's land?" He tossed his half-eaten apple into the garbage.

Karen jumped as the apple landed with a thud. Was she still so nervous? She remembered how she had stumbled off the bus, frightened that someone would catch her with Yasmine's lunchbox. She felt as if she were committing a crime. Yasmine, her face framed in the bus window, had nodded toward no man's land. Karen had understood exactly what Yasmine wanted her to do. This was their excuse if anyone caught them. They were switching back their lunchboxes.

But did she have the courage? No man's land separated her home and kibbutz from Yasmine's village. They lived in the only two settlements on top of a mountain that shared a border with Lebanon, yet the gap between them felt bigger than the whole Mediterranean Sea.

Karen shrugged off the fear. What was no man's land, after all? Just a four-mile field that lay between them, an empty plot left to grow wild, with both sides contesting it, wanting to claim it as their own. What could possibly happen to her?

"What about the ghosts?" asked David.

"Ghosts?" said Karen. "Those are just stupid stories to keep people away. Besides, if there were any ghosts haunting no man's land, they wouldn't come out in the afternoon. Everyone would see them and chase them away. Only babies believe in ghosts, David. You don't believe in them, do you?"

Pulling out his machine gun from his basket of war toys, David said, "I'm not a baby. I'm eight years old and I'm not afraid of anything." He cocked the gun and propped it up against his shoulder.

"Grow up, David," said Karen. But as usual, to humor him, she fell into step behind him as he marched out the door.

This time, though, she had an uneasy feeling. The game was a little too real. They were marching off to no man's land to meet the enemy—face to face.

CHAPTER 2
GUNFIRE!

Karen marched behind David along the winding paths of their kibbutz. She frowned at the dark clouds gathering over the grove.

"There's Joe," called David, waving. "He's still trying to replant the garden that got hit by a rocket last year. Maybe he should try plastic flowers for a change."

Karen bopped David on the head. "Don't be silly," she said. "Plastic roses wouldn't smell half as nice. You probably can't remember how Dad used to bring Mom fresh flowers every Friday. You were only four years old then."

"I do too remember. They used to make me sneeze." David scratched his nose. "I think I can still feel the tickle."

Karen laughed. "Dad used to say how nice it was to know that you could trust some things to never change."

"Like knowing that Mom will make chocolate cake every Friday," said David, licking his lips.

Karen kicked at an acorn, knowing David would chase after it. Her fingers tightened around the plastic handle of the lunchbox. She felt her insides somersaulting.

Sometimes it was good when things stayed the same. But what could be more exciting than the thrill of not knowing what was going to happen? She quickened her step in anticipation of meeting Yasmine.

"Race you to the grove!" yelled David.

Chasing after him, Karen dashed into the shade of the avocado grove at the edge of the kibbutz. She stopped under a large, thick tree to catch her breath. The avocado trees stood like leafy trolls guarding the border of no man's land. The daily noises of the kibbutz and the sweet, prickly odor of the chicken coops faded in the distance. No one was around except for a few blue jays and some crows. Suddenly a rumble in the distance broke the silence.

David grabbed her arm. "Gunfire!" he yelled. "Run for cover!"

Karen shook her arm free. "Calm down, silly, it's just thunder."

A flash of lightning broke through the dark clouds. David jumped. A long, low rumble followed.

"You have to listen for the difference," she said. Their dad had taught her. Now, she figured, since he wasn't around, it was her turn to teach David. "Gunfire," Karen explained, "makes a different sound. Like a woodpecker mistaking a metal pole for a pine tree."

David laughed. "Silly woodpecker."

The pecking sounds, Karen knew, were hollow and metallic and would ring in her ears even hours after the shooting had stopped.

David should have grown used to it by now. Karen couldn't recall a time when there weren't shots being fired off in the distance. Since they lived so close to Lebanon, where the war was still going on, their dad often said she should learn to listen and not jump at the thumping of her own heartbeat.

Some nights she and her dad would even stand outside and count the rockets shooting across the border. He could always tell who was firing on whom. Snuggled close to his chest, she'd watch the "fireworks," as she called them, until Mom forced them to come inside. "Don't worry so much, Barbie," he'd say. "It's miles away. Nothing can touch us."

Those noises hadn't bothered her. No, she thought, when she was David's age, no sound could have been worse than a hollering baby brother. But then the war came, and even David's screaming couldn't fill the emptiness.

"What's faster, Karie, an F-14 fighter plane or an F-16?" asked David.

"Well, I think—"

Before she could answer, he babbled on. "You know what I think? I think F-100s are the fastest, only they haven't built them yet. But when they do, I'm going to fly one, or maybe I'll build one. They've got super takeoff power and can zoom up and BOOM!" David threw down his gun into a pile of leaves and spread his arms out to show Karen how his bomber plane could soar and swoop and roar as it swept through the grove.

"Look, there's an avocado that got left on the tree." Shooting off, David swung up like a monkey into the branches, finally giving her a moment of quiet.

Under the cover of the broad avocado leaves, Karen felt like a wood nymph or an explorer in a thick jungle paradise. Her father, when he was first called to serve in the army, had said how beautiful it was in Lebanon, how untouched and like a Garden of Eden. He, too, felt like an explorer. "Even after being here for six months, sometimes I forget I'm not a tourist," he'd say with his deep baritone voice. "I always wish I had my camera instead of a gun."

That was at the beginning. Later, when Karen would ask him to tell her about all the sights, his eyes would grow dark. "It's hard to see beauty through the clouds of smoke," he would say. "And birds can't sing over the sound of gunfire."

Picking capers off a wild shrub, Karen peeled away the green pods and popped the inner flower buds in her mouth. Bitter, but tasty. She picked a few more and slipped them into her pocket.

All of a sudden a small green object came hurtling toward her.

"Bombs away!" shouted David.

"Ouch!" Karen jumped aside as another avocado came firing down. "David Silver, if you throw one more I'm going to mash you into avocado paste."

David shinnied down the trunk and took off between the trees. "Let's see if you really know how to run. I bet you can't catch me!"

Karen took off after him but let him dash ahead. David, so young and short, wasn't a problem to catch. It was sinewy kids like Yasmine, with mountain-goat legs and an unearthly swiftness, who would be hard to outrun. Yasmine was going to be her real competition in the next race. Like all her friends on the track team, Karen hadn't wanted Enrico, their coach, to let Arabs join the team. Soon, though, she had grown used to the dark, barefoot girls training beside her. She even found herself looking forward to running against them because winning against them was a double victory. And with the race only four weeks away, it was hard to think of anything else.

"You're pretty fast for having such puny legs," yelled Karen. She slowed her pace to let David get farther ahead.

"You can't catch me! You can't catch me!" David's singsong voice echoed through the trees like the cawing of the crows.

Karen chased behind him. Clutching Yasmine's lunchbox, she followed her brother through the avocado grove toward a hole in the barbed-wire fence, the entrance—if anyone was crazy enough to go in—to no man's land. As Karen reached David, he dove into a pile of leaves and came up holding his machine gun.

"I'm a commando soldier!" he shouted. "Come any closer and you're history!"

Before Karen could jump sideways, she heard a metal sound ring in her ears.

BOOM! BOOM! BOOM!

Without a second's hesitation, she dove in next to David under the thin cover of compost leaves.

CHAPTER 3
DEADLY MISTAKES

"Don't even breathe," Karen whispered. Wrapping her arms around David, she pulled him closer. "They won't find us if we're quiet."

"Isn't it just thunder?" David asked, his mouth close to her ear, his breath smelling faintly sour.

"Not this time," she said.

Karen inhaled long and deep, trying to breathe in the smell of the earth and calm the panic racing through her. She squeezed David even tighter, listening to the crushing of leaves and fallen twigs as footsteps moved toward them. She didn't dare swallow, afraid that even the smallest sound would give them away. Who would be out in the grove so late in the afternoon?

She shut her eyes to stay calm, but the nightmare came instead.

Ever since her father had been killed, the picture of him in his last few moments, alone in enemy territory, haunted her thoughts. She wondered what he had thought of before he died. What does someone think as danger approaches? Can you hear death? Smell it? Can you hide from it?

Only a week before he died, she overheard him telling her mother in a voice cracked and strained, "It has done something strange to me, Barbie. I've learned how easy it is to kill."

The words had hit Karen with a force that winded her. She had wanted to shut out the voices but had to hear the rest, to try to understand the soldier downstairs who suddenly sounded like a stranger.

"Are you surprised?" he had asked her mother. The silence had lasted for what felt like hours. "It's not hard to aim and shoot," he had said. "But it's the after-moment that surprises you, like the backfire of a jeep. It makes your legs tremble like a chicken on its way to the slaughter. It's the after-moment that kills something inside of you."

David's head jerked up, bumping Karen's chin. "He's coming closer," he whispered in her ear. Karen clapped her hand over David's mouth and shut her eyes again.

But instead of blackness came pictures of chickens. She had seen chickens with their heads lopped off. They ran around until the blood stopped spurting from their necks and they dropped down dead. Her stomach did a belly flop, and for a second she thought she might empty out her lunch on David. She gulped in air to calm her nerves and swallowed a hiccup.

David's hand felt hot and sticky in hers. Some brave commando soldier you are, she wanted to taunt him, but instead squeezed him even tighter, glad in a way that he was beside her, forcing her to feel strong.

"It'll be all right, David," she murmured in his ear. "Don't be scared. I'll protect you."

"You're hurting my hand," he sobbed.

A lump the size of an avocado pit wedged in Karen's throat, making breathing almost impossible. David buried his head in her lap, too terrified to look up.

"All right, kids, out you get," came a gruff voice. Slowly Karen raised her eyes. She would be brave for both of them, like her dad would have wanted her to be.

A strong hand wrapped around her wrist, wrenching her up. Karen dragged David out from the heap of dead leaves. "Don't shoot us," he begged.

Karen took a deep breath. Meeting their captor's eyes, she exhaled slowly and felt her legs go limp.

"It's only Joe, David. Stop sniveling! He's probably just here to irrigate the trees."

David peeked out from behind her and rubbed his eyes. He wiped his runny nose on her shirt.

"Aren't you a sight, soldier!" said Joe, brushing an empty, lifeless sleeve across David's face. He bent his gangly legs and picked up David, who was still shaking. "If you were an avocado sapling, I'd tie a good sturdy pole behind you," he said. "Now, tell me, what are you two rascals up to out here alone in the grove? If I know your mom, I'm sure she wouldn't like it. There's been gunfire across the border all day." Joe nodded out past Yasmine's village toward Lebanon.

David glanced up, pointed a shaking finger in the direction of the Arab village, and buried his head again. "You mean they're shooting at us?"

Joe laughed. "Why would they do that? They're our neighbors. They may not be exactly like us, but we've been living side by side for a long time. No, David. Our enemies are on the other side of the border, but maybe one day that, too, will change. In the meantime though, it isn't safe to wander out alone. What was it you were up to?"

"Nothing, Joe," said Karen. "David just wanted to look for some leftover avocados, and I wanted to train for the big race. If I'm going to win, I have to practice."

"I've heard about those lightning legs of yours. You've got your dad's running genes."

David, his head still buried in Joe's shoulder, mumbled, "The coach doesn't let them run in jeans. Shorts only."

Joe winked at Karen. "Is that so? Makes sense to me. Now, let's see how fast you two can run home." He put down David, who slipped his sweaty hand back into Karen's but didn't budge.

"Why did you shoot at us?" he asked. "Did you think we were enemy spies?"

Joe started to laugh, but somewhere along the way it got caught in his throat. He kneeled down to wipe David's snotty face with an avocado leaf. "No, David, I wouldn't ever shoot at you. It's those birds I'm after. Look, there's one. I don't want them picking at the few pear trees we've got tucked away in our grove. This isn't a gun with real bullets. It just makes noise that scares the birds away."

"But it scared me a little," said David. "And I'm training to be a soldier. I'm not supposed to get scared." He dropped his eyes to the ground, and his shoulders hunched forward. His machine gun still lay buried under the compost leaves.

Instead of pity, Karen couldn't check a growing feeling of annoyance. "Grow up, David. You're acting like a baby. Pick up your gun, and we'll go home."

"Don't be so hard on him, Karen," said Joe. "I'll tell you a secret, David, soldier-to-soldier." Fishing out the gun, he handed it back to David. "Four years ago, when your dad was my commanding officer, he gave me a piece of advice I'll never forget. He said that a really good soldier is always a little afraid. It makes him careful and on the watch for danger." He paused and looked up at Karen. "Because danger can be lurking anywhere." Joe slapped David on the back. "You take good care of your sister. And that's an order, soldier!"

David smiled, but didn't salute.

"Bye, Joe," said Karen, turning toward home. "Next time I'll come on my own," she mumbled, "if there is a next time."

Dragging his gun barrel through the dust, David left a thin path in the dirt. He looked like a defeated soldier on his way home. Now she'd have to give him something to eat and play with him to keep him from telling Mom what happened. At least David had been too distracted to tell Joe about Yasmine's lunchbox.

"The lunchbox," she said suddenly. "I've left it in the leaves. Wait here, David, I'll be right back."

Before David could object, she ran back toward the pile of leaves. As she drew near, she saw Joe staring at Yasmine's tattered purple lunchbox.

"Don't come any closer!" he shouted. "This looks suspicious. It might be a bomb. Get yourself home quickly, and take David away from here." He waved at her with his good arm, the other sleeve flapping in the wind.

"But, Joe—"

"Don't argue, girl, it looks dangerous. There's some Arab writing on it. It might explode any minute. Get going now! That's an order."

CHAPTER 4
PEANUT BUTTER AND
JELLY EXPLOSION

"Did you hear it explode?"

Karen tugged David by the arm. "Come on, we have to get home."

"Like sitting on a thundercloud," he said, pushing Karen away to join Ellah, his best friend. "I thought my eardrums would split like lightning, but I still stayed and watched the *whole* thing," he bragged. "Let go, Karen, I have to tell Ellah all about it."

As if there were nothing else to talk about, thought Karen, annoyed at them all. Everyone kept going on about the box found in the field and how it had to be detonated. It had been blown up just in case it was a bomb made to look like a lunchbox. Karen hadn't wanted to watch, but not even a promise of an ice-cream soda would bribe David into leaving the scene.

So she had stayed with him as the bomb squad came tearing up the mountain with its sirens wailing. The robot—a little automated machine-man on wheels with long metal arms—toddled out, lifted up the suspicious package, and dumped it into an explosive-proof van. The crowd went wild. David's friends, dying to give an eyewitness report, tried to get as close as they could, only to be pushed out of the way by their parents, who wanted to see as well. And David, who had completely forgotten that he and Karen were the ones who had left the lunchbox in the first place, got all wrapped up in the excitement of playing the brave sapper and became David Silver, expert detonator of deadly devices.

Karen knew the box would be blown up—something about neutralizing any explosives inside, like setting a fire in the forest to stop the spread of an oncoming fire. The fires burnt each other out. The bombs blew each other up. It's what they always did. As she walked home with David, Karen imagined what would have happened if it had been her lunchbox they'd blown up. If it were Monday or Thursday, a cheese and tomato sandwich would have exploded on impact. Disgusting. But worse would have been a Tuesday or Wednesday, when she made her own lunch of peanut butter and jelly with bananas.

She had always laughed about blown-up homework assignments in abandoned schoolbags and knew that anything suspicious had to be investigated. You couldn't just open it first and take the risk of triggering it. Though she had tried to explain how the lunchbox had gotten there in the first place, no one wanted to listen to her, and she was afraid of being blamed for causing a false alarm, or even worse, getting Yasmine into trouble.

"A lunchbox," her mother said, shaking her head as Karen trudged into the house. "It's just too terrible to think of. And so close this time. I mean, who would even think of looking in our very own fields. There has to be a way to stop it. We just can't go on living like this."

"Mom, it's not what you think."

But Mrs. Silver had already turned her back on Karen to do the breakfast dishes. She resoaped the soapy ones, scrubbed at the clean ones, and tossed the dirty cutlery into the garbage. Karen had to dig around half-eaten peaches and soggy sandwiches to fish them out and dump them back into the sink.

"Karen, I don't want to talk about it. Just when I had David sleeping in his bed again. I know this is going to make him regress to more nights behind the couch."

Karen groaned. "Mom, when are you going to realize that it's perfectly normal for eight-year-old kids to sleep behind the couch? It's his fortress, and that's what boys do. They practice to be soldiers so that when they grow up they can go out and fight the real enemy like their dads do."

"I still think he could have a better hobby. I used to make things from rope—macramé we called it. I made a hammock once, and a plant hanger." She glanced proudly at Karen.

"Give David a piece of rope and he'll probably tie someone to a tree to interrogate them," said Karen.

Her mother frowned. "Then maybe we should try and get him to collect bugs. He loves those things."

Karen laughed and ducked to avoid being drenched as bubbles, water, and sponges flew into frantic motion.

When her mom threw herself into a cleaning frenzy, Karen knew she was thinking about how different life would be if only there were peace.

Karen sighed loudly enough for her mother to hear and stood by the kitchen doorway. "If only the psychologist could see *you* now," she said. "It would make David and me look a lot more normal."

Her mother snorted and threw a dishtowel at her. "I've no patience for your smart comments," she said. "We're a perfectly normal family; it's the world that's crazy. Go do some homework, or dry the dishes. You should be working harder at school instead of spending your time running around. David told me that you were out in the avocado grove again today."

Karen pulled up a chair and flopped down. "Mom, I'm training for the race and I have to practice as much as I can. Dad said I would be ready to compete when I was thirteen. So nothing you can say will stop me. Save your breath."

Karen barely flinched at the sound of a plate breaking in the sink and watched her mother gather up the pieces.

"If things get any worse, we'll need a new set of dishes by the end of the month," Mrs. Silver said, tossing the plate into the garbage. She picked up the next dish and held it more carefully. Keeping her back to Karen, she said, "Your dad shouldn't have encouraged you. You've got my short legs. We aren't built to be runners, not that your father listened to me then, either." She sighed, wiping her forehead with the back of her arm. "Did David save you any cake?"

Karen picked at the few remaining crumbs of cake. "I'm not hungry," she said, pushing away the plate. "And a lot of runners are short. It's speed, not height, that matters."

Her mother shrugged. "You should find a safer hobby, like macramé. I might have some rope left lying around somewhere." She dried her hands on a dishtowel and sat down opposite Karen. "I don't like you running through the grove. Who knows what could happen?"

Karen's answer was muffled by David charging out of his bedroom and running downstairs. "You missed all the fun!" he shouted. "I'm going to work on the bomb squad when I get old enough."

"Over my dead body!" said their mother.

As David dove behind the couch to barricade himself, Karen got up and slipped out the door.

The sounds of the sirens had faded, and everything seemed back to normal. Ellah's mother was yelling at her to finish her homework. Joe had turned on the sprinklers, and Karen had to dodge between them. Not much of the sun was left, as if it, too, was tired from all the excitement. Living on a kibbutz with the same people all your life, there weren't many surprises. Or perhaps it was just the opposite. You were waiting to be taken by surprise—by terrorists infiltrating from across the border, or by rockets shot off suddenly in the dead of night, or by fathers and neighbors who never came home. You were so used to waiting for surprises that they became kind of ordinary and the ordinary became a surprise.

Karen didn't waste much time thinking about it. She was worried about Yasmine. What was she going to tell her? "I'm sorry, your lunchbox was blown up," or, "Those hot chili peppers you guys like to eat were a blast." Nothing sounded right. She walked slowly toward the kibbutz store, hoping that there were still a few lunchboxes lying around among the food and household provisions.

Listening as the last squad car sped down the mountain, she wondered if Yasmine would want to start all over again. But deep down inside Karen had a feeling that with a start like this, things could only get worse.

CHAPTER 5
FATE ON THE BALANCE

The local bus lurched to a stop and the doors swung open.

"Grab the last seat or do the dance of death!" shouted Tami. "Fahad's behind the wheel."

Karen whipped around the pole as Fahad pulled away from the curb for their bungee-jumping ride down the mountain. Life was too short for Fahad. Wiggling impatiently in his seat, he gripped the steering wheel with his brown nail-bitten fingers as the bus flew over potholes and spun wildly around the curves.

"It's O.K., you grab the seat, Tami," said Karen. "I'll dance."

"It's not fair!" Tami complained loudly. "They always get picked up first. They get all the places to sit, and we have to stand." She pushed her way through to the last remaining seat next to Shira, one of their track teammates. "It's bad enough that we share the mountain with them, but the bus, too?"

"Quit crowding me, Tami," said Shira.

Karen elbowed her way down the middle of the bus, wishing that Tami didn't have to talk so loudly. Most of the Arab kids understood Hebrew, and besides, Tami's biting tone said even more than the words themselves. Karen stood in the center of the bus. Yasmine, looking straight ahead, pretended not to see her, but Karen was sure she was aware of her every move.

Karen wanted to say something to her but knew it was impossible. She noticed that Yasmine had arranged her hair differently. Three strands were woven tightly together and fastened with a colorful threaded ribbon. Karen would have liked to tell her how nice it looked.

"Hold on!" someone hollered as Fahad swerved, narrowly missing a donkey driver carrying a load of hay.

"Get out of my lap, you idiot!" Tami screeched as a dark-haired boy fell on top of her. She jumped up, grabbing the pole beside Karen. "At least our school is first and we get off this bus before they do," she said. "Why can't our school have its own bus? As if it's our fault that we live in such a godforsaken part of the country."

"Watch the curve!" shouted Shira.

Karen lost her balance and went reeling toward Yasmine's seat. She bent down as if to break her fall.

Inches from her hand, tucked under the seat, was her own lunchbox. She reached out for it, but just as her hand touched the familiar handle a big brown-sandaled foot came crashing down near her. Karen jerked back.

"What do you think you're doing?" asked Rana, who was sitting behind Yasmine.

Karen backed away. Tami swung around the pole. "She can do whatever she wants. You don't own the bus, you know."

Karen glanced at Yasmine, who was chewing on the inside of her lip. Her eyes darted nervously between Karen and Tami.

"Forget it, Tami," said Karen. "It's no big deal. I just lost my balance." The handle of the new lunchbox grew sweaty in her palm.

"Yeah," said Rana, "no big deal. But I saw you trying to snatch Yasmine's lunchbox."

Karen froze. She didn't dare look at Yasmine. She clutched the handle of the box tighter. Her other hand tensed around the pole. Now what? How was she going to get out of this? All the kids around them had fallen silent. All those eyes staring at her. Karen glanced at the new box in her hand. She had chosen it because it had looked like one Yasmine would have wanted. Around the rim were stars. Not Jewish stars, but five-pointed stars, like the ones in the sky that belonged to both of them.

"Rana," said Yasmine softly but firmly, "be quiet. You don't know what you're talking about."

Karen drew in a deep breath. Their secret was out. But before anyone could say another word, Tami's roaring laugh shattered the stillness. She tossed her hair back, and her shoulders shook. "As if Karen would want that smelly old thing!" she said. "She's got a new one! Come on, Karen. I don't want to waste any more of my time on them."

Fahad made another turn, and Tami lunged desperately for the pole.

"Fahad, watch the curve!"

"He's going to kill us!" someone shouted.

Tami collided into Karen and giggled. "Did you hear about the bomb yesterday?" she asked.

Karen avoided Tami's eyes. "How do you know it was a bomb?"

"What else could it have been?"

Karen shrugged. "Maybe someone's lunch?"

Tami laughed again. Her answer was drowned out by Fahad slamming on the brakes and screeching to a stop.

"We don't have much time today," he said as he grudgingly opened the door. "The kids are already late." He drummed his fingers on the gearshift, ready to plunge forward.

"I won't be long," the Israeli soldier answered. "It's just routine. After that suspicious package yesterday, we can't be too careful."

Karen saw the top of the soldier's short-cropped hair as he jumped up onto the first step. He wore army fatigues and had to duck when he reached the top stair. Around his waist was a matching olive belt, and swinging over his shoulder, a machine gun. David would know its name. He knew the name of every bomber plane and every rifle.

To Karen, naming a gun was like giving it a life of its own, when all it really brought was death. Her father had tried to explain the love-hate relationship he had with his gun, but she could never understand. She hated the cold, stained metal and the way it dangled over her father's shoulder like a dead arm.

"I hope he takes a long time and makes us late for history," whispered Tami. "I didn't finish my homework."

Nodding and smiling at the kids, the soldier made his way through the bus, all the while pointing at every bag to see whom it belonged to, making sure that there was nothing suspicious and no unclaimed packages.

The air on the crowded bus grew heavy, and Karen felt suffocated. She linked eyes with Yasmine. It was like staring at an inside-out picture of herself. As light as her own hair was, Yasmine's was dark. Karen's eyes, seemingly streaked by the sun, couldn't have been lighter than the black of Yasmine's. Karen listened as the soldier made his way down the aisle of the bus, the metal of his gun clinking against the seats.

She remembered how her father would tell her about the multitude of sounds he heard on night patrols, and the constant fear of never knowing which noises shouldn't be there. "Picking out the sounds in the darkness is like playing pin the tail on the donkey at night with a blindfold," he'd say. "It doesn't help to peek." Karen wondered if the sounds on the bus were any different. They were surely just as heavy with unspoken fears.

Tami tore the paper off a chocolate bar. "Want some?" she asked.

Karen shook her head. "I've sworn off chocolate until after the track race," she said, her eyes following the soldier's every step.

He stopped beside Yasmine's seat. "Are those yours?" he asked, pointing to her schoolbag and Karen's lunchbox.

Karen froze. If Yasmine even flinched he would suspect something, and then Tami and everyone would know about them. Karen didn't want to stare, but she couldn't will herself to turn away.

Yasmine nodded. She smiled as if everything was as it should be, incredibly calm. Karen wiped her sweaty palms on her pant leg.

The soldier moved on.

For Yasmine, the danger didn't come from a soldier with a gun, thought Karen, but from the other Arab kids. They would be suspicious of her for befriending someone like Karen, someone from the other side. They would be angry at her for drawing attention to them. Suspect her of stirring up trouble. Just as Tami would accuse Karen of being a traitor and betraying her real friends.

It's like when you weighed yourself the morning before a track race, Karen thought. As long as you were careful not to eat any chocolate snacks, the scales remained balanced. There was the same delicate balance between Jews and Arabs. But a little thing, like she and Yasmine switching lunchboxes, could upset the balance. People would start wondering who's right and who's wrong.

Or if there ever was a right or wrong.

CHAPTER 6
ABDULLAH

After making his rounds on the bus, the soldier gave Fahad a mock salute and Fahad slammed the doors shut behind him. Karen grabbed hold of the pole, ready for takeoff. She didn't dare look at Yasmine, afraid she would give away their secret.

But suddenly Karen felt strangely uneasy. Slowly turning around, she glanced over her shoulder. And that's when she saw him, a tall, thin, brown-haired boy with black bullet eyes and sunbaked skin.

As she tried to figure out who he was, their eyes met. He didn't flinch. Didn't look away. Taking in her white blouse, her faded blue jeans, and her light frizzy hair, he fixed his glare on her anxious hazel eyes.

Unashamed that she had caught him staring, he boldly scrutinized her. Fighting the urge to look aside, afraid to falter, and not wanting him to win, Karen stared back. Their eyes were polar magnets, with a force both repelling them, yet keeping them fixed.

As the bus veered around a curve, Karen moved with it, and the moment between them was gone. Who is he? she wondered. Something about his almond-shaped lips reminded her of Yasmine. He had to be Yasmine's older brother. And then she remembered overhearing Enrico talk about him. "The boy runs like a mountain goat," he had said, "swiftly and gracefully." Abdullah, Enrico had called him. Arrogant Abdullah. She had heard his nickname from some of the boys in her class.

A pang of fear sent a shiver through Karen, and she turned away. Had he been spying on them? Did he know? He had surely heard Rana's exchange with Tami. Karen brushed the sweat from her brow. She could feel trouble brewing and wondered what shape it would take. She took a deep breath as the bus pulled up to her school.

Karen got off the bus, but Abdullah's look stayed with her. She went through the rest of the day with a feeling of uneasiness. History. Math. English and Hebrew. And the whole time she just wanted to get to the track.

She needed to run. Needed to run to forget about Abdullah's eyes. Were those the eyes that haunted her dad? When he came home on leave from the army, he would tell her how eerie it was to feel that his every move was being watched. He would pull on his track suit and say, "I'll run with you another day, Karen. Right now I have to run out those eyes." But he had never come back to run with her, and she was left to train alone.

"Karen! Hurry," called Tami. "You'll be late for track, and Enrico will have a fit!"

"I'm trying to, but Mr. Meyers wouldn't let us out of class. It's bad enough that we have him six days a week. The least he could do is let us out on time!" She kicked off her sandals and tugged open her schoolbag. "Some of these teachers think we would sit there all day if we could!"

Tami laughed. "Who wouldn't rather be on the track than in a hot, stuffy classroom?" She dug a pebble from her shoe. "But one of these days they better find us a normal field to run on."

Looking critically at the track, Karen had to agree. "I wonder how much longer we'll even be able to use this field before they start building the new school?"

Tami shrugged. "It's always the same story. We find empty land to run on, and then someone remembers that there were plans for it and *we* have to move on. But my dad is joining the local planning committee, so we'll probably have a new place soon. Haven't you even got your shoes on yet?"

Karen turned her schoolbag upside down. "I know they're in here somewhere."

Tami tapped her foot impatiently. "If you can't find your shoes, run barefoot like the Arab girls," she said, and laughed.

"How they run so fast over the rocks and roots without shoes on, I don't know," said Karen, triumphantly pulling her shoes from the bag and emptying out a pencil sharpener and her lost eraser from one of them.

"You don't know how they do it?" said Tami. "Well, I don't know why they do it!"

Karen finished tying her laces. "They do it because they want to run, just like we do. Maybe they can't afford fancy running shoes like we can, or maybe they're used to running barefoot, but either way they are good runners."

Tami snorted. "So what? Who ever heard of mixing Arabs and Israelis on the same team? My parents weren't the only ones who complained, you know. But that Enrico is so stubborn, do you know what he said?"

Karen knew. It was what he always said when parents complained. "'I don't work at the United Nations. I'm a coach, not a diplomat.'"

"That's right," said Tami. "If he weren't the best track coach in our area, I'd find another team to train with. Those Arab girls know nothing about team spirit. They only stick with each other." Tami dropped her voice to a whisper. "And whenever they whisper, I get the feeling they're conspiring against us."

"Maybe you could teach them to be friendlier," said Karen, avoiding the look of disgust she was sure Tami shot her.

Tami snorted again and took a few steps away from her. "Not all of us want to be buddy-buddy with Arabs, Karen. I've seen the way you look at them—we all have. But just watch out! It won't do you any good. Learn who your real friends are and don't mix with them, or you'll regret it." She continued to edge away, leaving Karen alone by the side of the track.

CHAPTER 7
RUNNING ON ANGER

"Nice of you to show up!" Enrico bellowed as Karen joined the group. "I expect my runners to be on the track on time. We've got a race less than one month away, and you had better be in shape." He studied them carefully one after the other, a frown tugging at the corners of his mouth. "In this year's Galilee Run, the first three runners will determine the team's time, and those will be the runners who come with me for the 10K in Spain this summer. Is that clear?"

"Olé!" Tami whispered to Karen.

Enrico silenced her with a scowl. "I expect the best from all of you. The sports council will sponsor the winners, but only if I think you're good enough to go and represent us!"

He blew his whistle long and loud. "One kilometer warmup!" he shouted as they took off. "Build up slowly. Next three kilometers you run with all you've got!"

Karen sped up.

"Easy, Karen," said Tami, running up beside her. "We're supposed to take this one slowly."

Karen nodded. "Enrico seems grumpier than usual today. I wonder what's bugging him?"

"He's just being his usual charming self," said Tami, and giggled.

But Karen had the feeling that something wasn't right. It wasn't just Enrico's quick temper. She looked around to see if anyone else had noticed and realized that two girls were missing. One of them was Yasmine.

"Looking for your buddy?" asked Tami, matching Karen step for step.

"She's not my buddy, Tami, so just quit it, O.K.?" But Yasmine was never late for track. There had to be a reason. Karen tried to distance herself from Tami.

"Maybe she's too scared to run against me in my new shoes and has chickened out," said Tami, closing the gap between them.

Karen glanced at Tami's shoes as they hit the ground beside hers. "You wish. You still have a long way to go before you could ever beat her."

Karen continued to keep watch for Yasmine, but when there was still no sign of her after they had finished the warmup lap, she gave up looking. Yasmine wasn't coming.

"Without that Arab girl, at least now I know I'll come in first today," said Tami. "These new shoes my dad bought me are supposed to be the best. They've got air pockets and special balancing pads." She sped ahead as Enrico blew his whistle.

"This isn't a tea party! Stop talking and start running!" he shouted.

Karen took off. The frustrations and anger of the day boiling inside her gave her the steam to run. She sprinted forward, trying to ignore the pain in her right side that stabbed her with each step. The air burned her throat. Tami fell a few lengths behind her, but on the last lap, with four hundred meters to go, Tami dashed past her. Karen watched helplessly as Tami, in her new running shoes, beat her across the finish line.

Enrico clocked them in, crossed his arms, and drummed his fingers on his bulging biceps. His hair, usually fixed in a long ponytail, had come loose. He frowned at Karen.

"Sorry, Enrico, my head was just somewhere else and my side was hurting."

"The way you were pounding the ground it looked like you were getting ready for a boxing match, not a track race. You've got to spring off the ground, not batter it. With this team getting smaller every day, I wonder if there's any point." He frowned and for a moment a look of defeat crossed his face. Then he turned back to Karen and said defiantly, "Don't waste your time, Karen, and don't waste mine!"

"I'll be ready for the race, Enrico, I promise." She rested her hands on her knees.

Enrico drew closer. "You have to learn to relax," he said, his breath smelling faintly of garlic. "Concentrate, Karen. Focus. I want to see your eyes, your jaw, your shoulders, hands and hips all relaxed. Do you understand me?" Karen nodded, feeling too winded to speak.

"Good, because running needs total concentration. Listen to your breathing. Listen to your heart. Listen to every vein in your body as it pumps and contracts. Just don't listen to that head of yours and all those mixed-up thoughts. Anger won't get you going any faster."

Looking up he waved off the rest of the girls. "One kilometer cooldown and then you're all dismissed," he called.

"I'll stay for a bit longer, if that's all right," said Karen.

Enrico looked at her, narrowing his eyes and twitching his mustache. "Fine by me. Just don't miss the bus home."

As she rounded her last lap, Karen saw a familiar figure in the distance. Her heartbeat quickened, and a surge of adrenaline pumped through her. She lifted her chin, threw back her shoulders, and focused on the finish line. She'd whip past Yasmine and Enrico so fast they'd think they'd caught only the tail end of a comet.

But as she drew closer, she heard Enrico's voice, loud and angry. He had his hands deep in his pockets and was pacing furiously.

"I can't believe this! First Suma and now you! I'm not running a brothel—this is a track team. No one is looking at your bony legs. They're watching the clock and timing your speed. You tell your father that, O.K.? Because I can't have my runners skipping around in skirts. Either you wear what all runners wear, or you're off the team. Shorts. T-shirt. I don't care if you wear shoes or not, but don't start preaching to me about modesty and your ancient customs. We've got a race to win. You girls win this race, and we'll be on the map. I train world-class runners, not ballerinas in tutus!"

Yasmine, her head bowed, mumbled something Karen couldn't hear. Neither Yasmine nor Enrico noticed her as she slowed down and walked toward the finish line.

"I could be coaching anywhere in the world, but I chose here!" shouted Enrico even louder. "You know why?"

Karen couldn't hear Yasmine's response, but she knew his answer by heart.

"That's right! Because you kids have some untapped talent. I don't know if it's the mountain air, the rugged terrain, or the fear of death behind every tree, but you kids were born to run. I'll make this the best track team in the country, even in the world." He paused and raised his arms to the sky. "You're my best runner, Yasmine. But I can only take you to the top if you run by my rules."

Yasmine fled from the course, her skirt catching the wind and her sobs echoing in the still, hot air.

Looking over at Enrico, Karen shuddered. She had never seen him so angry. Enrico, who wasn't a Jew or an Arab, couldn't understand either side. He pushed the Arab girls into wearing running uniforms, just as he pushed Tami into sharing the starting line with girls she wouldn't share a word with. He wanted his runners and their communities to work as a team, to make running their common religion.

Karen sighed. Some things could never change. And because of Enrico's stubbornness, Yasmine had to drop off the team. Why wouldn't he let them run in skirts? It wasn't

Yasmine's fault. Karen suspected it was probably Abdullah's doing.

She looked over their makeshift racecourse and felt an awkward sense of loneliness. It wouldn't be the same running without Yasmine. They would all start side by side, but soon she and Yasmine would leave the other girls behind. Yasmine was fast, and Karen loved the challenge of trying to outrun her. She sighed again. She'd miss the competition.

She took a long drink of water, building up the nerve to challenge Enrico. "Would it be so bad if the Arab girls ran in skirts?" she asked, wiping the sweat from her brow.

Enrico looked at her, frustration still simmering in his eyes. "Don't be ridiculous. It would add minutes to her time, and I'm not running a comedy troupe. Run by my rules, or not at all."

"But it's not Yasmine's fault that she can't wear shorts." Karen pursed her lips together. "I bet her brother's behind all this. He doesn't want her around us. Enrico, he's ruining everything!" She kicked at a pebble, sending up a cloud of dust.

Enrico shook his head and waved away the dust. "I wish it were that easy. Throw the blame on someone else. We may not like it, but it's their culture." He twitched his mustache into one of his rare smiles. "You worry about yourself, Karen. You've got to practice every day. You can win this race if you keep your mind focused. It's too bad Yasmine won't be around anymore. She got the fire under your feet burning."

Karen rolled back her shoulders and looked Enrico straight in the eye. She couldn't let him think that Yasmine was that important to her.

"I don't need Yasmine's help to win the race," she said. "I can do it on my own."

Enrico scooped his hair back and tied his ponytail tighter. "Good, because in these next few weeks I expect you all to train on your own. Running this track three times a week is not enough to keep you in shape, and there isn't much time left before school ends and before the race. Hopefully we'll have the new track by then. In the meantime, you and the girls must keep training." He glanced wistfully around the track.

"I can do it," she promised. "I can win it."

"It takes a lot of self-discipline to train alone," Enrico said. "Which is what you'll have to do these next few weeks. It's lonely and grueling work." And as if reading her mind, he said, "Somewhere inside you is the talent to be a winner, Karen, as long as you have the determination and self-control."

CHAPTER 8
A HOLE IN THE FENCE

"Hello! Anybody home? I—" Karen stopped. "Oh, hi, Ben. You're here, too?"

Ben smiled at her and blushed. "Hello, Karen. Your mother and I both decided to leave work early today and finish up the odds and ends later. How's the running going?" He put his coffee mug on the table. "You're looking fit."

"Fine," Karen answered. She dumped her schoolbag by the door and began planning her fastest means of escape. She had been waiting all day to come home and throw on her track clothes. The last thing she wanted was to waste time making small talk with her mom's boyfriend.

Her mother came out of the kitchen carrying a plate of cookies. "Hi, Karen. Are you hungry?"

"No thanks, Mom. You know I can't eat that stuff until after the race."

"My daughter the runner," she said, rolling her eyes and smiling at Ben. "I wish I had her will power. Why don't you sit down with us and talk for a bit, Karen? Ben's brought some book on bugs to show David."

Ben laughed. "I can see by the look on your face that you're not interested in entomology." He smiled at Karen. "It's just a little hobby of mine. Your mother thought David might enjoy collecting ants."

"David, an ant collector?" Karen shrugged. What would her mother think of next? Summoning up every bit of self-control, she smiled through clenched teeth. "Sounds like a super idea, Ben. I'd love to stay and hear more, but I've got to change for my run. We don't have track on Tuesdays, and I have to be in shape."

"Don't run off, Karen. Stay and talk with us for a while."

Talk, thought Karen. Talk about what? "Sorry, Mom, maybe another time. I have to hurry if you want me back before dark."

She ran up the stairs, closing her bedroom door firmly behind her. Now she really needed to run, and far. As she tore off her school clothes, she listened to her mother bustling about the living room, probably smoothing her dress, arranging the trinkets on their coffee table, making small talk about Karen and David as if they were a normal family.

But somewhere inside Karen didn't feel normal at all. Stay and talk. The words had sounded so strange. They hadn't talked for ages, not really, anyway. Not like they used to. She didn't remember when she and her mother stopped talking. But ever since her dad hadn't been around, they just kept on passing each other by, assuming that things were forgotten, or better left unsaid. The psychologist had said that it would take them awhile to readjust and fill in the empty spaces. As if the empty space in their lives could be colored in like a paint-by-number.

Karen slipped out of the house unnoticed. Ben and her mother were deep in conversation, as if her mother had years of silence to make up for. Karen craved the stillness. At least the avocado grove would be empty, and quiet, she thought, with no one asking her to talk or share. Just like her dad, Karen loved to run alone.

But once in the grove, Karen realized that it was impossible to train there. Joe had begun to lay down irrigation lines, and the thin black pipes stretching from tree to tree got tangled between her feet and interrupted the pace of her run. She needed an empty field, with no irrigation pipes and no sprinklers popping out of the ground every few feet.

Without actually planning to, Karen found herself standing by the hole in the fence and looking out wistfully into the open space of no man's land. The rugged freedom of the turf seemed to call her. The trees, their branches like open arms, beckoned her forward, waiting to envelop her. The uncultivated field, left to grow wild while caught in the dispute of who really owned it, seemed peaceful and unaware of the problems it was causing. Karen took a deep breath, wondering if Yasmine had gazed at the field from her side, feeling the same temptation she felt now. Quickly, before she could convince herself not to, she slipped through the hole and found herself on the other side.

Small shrubs of sage grew in bunches by the fence. She broke off a branch, and the air swelled with its strong odor. She saw a few wild poppies and some red oleanders that were just beginning to blossom. After tightening her shoelaces, she started to run. At first she kept the pace slow since the terrain was unfamiliar and rocky in patches. Beating down the weeds with each step, she plotted a path.

Karen ran patiently, placing each foot securely, as if with each step she was claiming no man's land for her own. Listening to the sound of her feet as they touched the untrampled land, she inhaled the delicate aroma of the wild brush. The crickets hidden in the grass chirped. The wind blew through her hair. The silence that was not silence but the sounds of nature thriving and wild. If she trained here over the next three weeks, she would be able to beat them all and take the race. She would be Enrico's star athlete and prove to her mother that she was a runner and could be what her father wanted her to be.

She followed an almost natural path as it wound between two olive trees and one knobby pistachio tree. Farther on was an almond tree, but it was the kind with bitter fruit, so she didn't stop to pick any. Just before the path headed down a slope, a panoramic view of Yasmine's village lit up the rocky landscape, the houses trimmed with bright turquoise and green to ward off the evil eye and bring good luck. Once the path dipped downward, tall pine trees with prickly needles obscured everything, and Karen was left to focus on the weed- and rock-covered path beneath her feet.

Karen had never felt so free. For the first time in her life she was without walls, soldiers to guard her, or wire fences. Like the birds that flew above or the weeds that crawled through any crevice, nothing could hold her back.

She ran on. Sweat gathered on her brow and trickled down the sides of her face. Her feet pounded the earth in rhythm with her breathing—she would inhale sharply, her side stinging, and exhale. The gentle breeze blowing through her hair and slipping through the sleeves of her shirt cooled her chest and prickled her skin.

She ran on, distracted for a moment by a play of shadows that seemed to follow her own. And then, before she could decide whether anything had really been there or not, it disappeared into the shade of a tree.

"Go away, ghosts!" she called. She wasn't scared. The land was free. But she couldn't shake off the feeling that she was not alone. She thought perhaps it was the spirit of her father, chasing behind her, slipping in front of her. She imagined him running beside her in awkward ministrides, shouting, "Come on, lightning legs, push harder!"

Karen picked up speed. All her thoughts focused on the run.

Suddenly, as she rounded a bend, she bumped straight into someone and let out a scream that shattered the silence and sent the birds up in a frightened confusion of wings. Karen had collided headfirst into a ghost!

CHAPTER 9
RUNNING ON EGGS

"What? You! What are you doing here?" Karen stumbled backward, trying to catch her breath, clutching her chest to calm her heartbeat.

Yasmine hopped on one foot. "You've stepped on my toe. Why don't you watch where you're going?"

"How was I supposed to know you were going to come swinging around the corner like Fahad on a bad day? You scared the living daylights out of me!"

Karen stared at Yasmine. She looked so different without her school uniform on. A faded purple skirt clung to her long legs, and her face dripped with sweat. She watched as Yasmine bent down, brushing strands of hair from her face and wiping her brow with the hem of her skirt.

"I didn't mean to scare you. But you startled me!" said Yasmine.

Karen eyed her curiously. "How did you get in here?"

Yasmine turned and started to walk. "We'd better keep moving or our muscles will tense up."

Karen fell in beside her, careful to leave enough space between them.

"We have a little hole on our side of the fence," Yasmine explained. "No one ever comes in here, though. I found it one day when I was looking for almonds and knew it was just for me. I figured that if I ran here, my father would never find out, and I'd be safe."

Karen plucked a blade of lemon grass to chew on. Yasmine had come to no man's land to run alone, away from everyone else, just as she had. Karen smiled to herself.

"We have a hole on our side of the fence, too," said Karen. They walked on, keeping an easy pace. "It's too bad you had to drop off the track team," she added. "It was fun running against you."

Yasmine smiled. "Against me? I thought we were on the same team." She stopped walking, and Karen saw her smile fade. "I could have beaten you all," she said. "But my father won't let me train anymore. He says it's immodest to run in shorts."

"But that other Arab girl—what's her name—she runs in shorts."

"Rana?" Yasmine's laugh was high and jittery and seemed to jump out of her like a surprised rabbit.

"What's so funny?" asked Karen.

Yasmine shrugged. "Her father is not well-liked in our community. They think he is too progressive and is ruining his daughter's status. A girl like that, they say, will never get a husband. It's not true, though. Rana is very modest, and serious. And she's a good runner. You'll have to work hard to beat her. I could have beaten her, though. Watch that root." Karen scooted around an upturned root not far from the hole in the fence leading to the avocado grove. She stopped to pick up her water bottle. She took a sip and offered it to Yasmine.

Yasmine drank some and handed back the bottle. Her smile was overshadowed again, and Karen knew she was thinking about the race. "Maybe next year you'll be able to race," she said.

"Maybe," said Yasmine. Then grabbing Karen by the hand, she said, "But this year I will help you train! You need a lot of help."

Karen felt her cheeks flush. Yasmine thought she wasn't good enough. "I'm doing fine," she said, removing her hand from Yasmine's grip. "Enrico says I just need a little more practice."

Yasmine grunted. "Fine is not good enough." She looked critically at Karen. "Take those off," she said, pointing to her running shoes.

"My running shoes? Why should I?"

"The way you pound the earth in them, I'm surprised you haven't reached the other side."

Karen looked down at her running shoes. They had cost a fortune, a birthday present from her mom. Then she looked at Yasmine's brown feet, covered with scrapes and marked by a black toenail.

"Listen, Yasmine, I'm not like you. I'd kill myself running barefoot. Besides, just because you run without shoes doesn't mean it's better, it's just different."

Yasmine folded her arms across her chest and stuck out her chin. "Have you ever tried swimming a race without water?"

Karen raised her eyebrows. "Of course not! I wouldn't get anywhere flapping my arms and legs around if there wasn't water."

"Just my point," said Yasmine. "If you can't feel the earth under your feet, then you end up flapping about in those fancy shoes without knowing what's beneath you."

Karen shook her head. Sitting down on a rock, she tugged off her shoes. "I must be crazy," she mumbled. "What about thorns, rocks, and twigs?"

"Don't worry. You've been pounding this course so hard that it will probably be like running on feathers once you take your shoes off. Come on, we'll do this next lap together."

Karen assumed her starting position.

"Take the first round slowly," Yasmine coached. "Try and keep your breathing rhythmic. It's still hot, so don't push too fast."

"Barefoot," mumbled Karen, wiggling her toes and feeling the prickly, dry grass against her soles. "This is not going to work."

"Don't be so negative," said Yasmine. "You'll never know what can happen if you don't take a chance. It works great for me."

Karen took off, feeling Yasmine slow her pace so as not to outrun her. "Ouch!" she hollered as her foot brushed against a protruding root. "My toenail!" she screamed a few yards later as she stubbed it against a rock. Finally, after a painful lap, she managed to hobble across the finish line.

Yasmine, Karen saw, was trying hard not to laugh. "Sorry, Karen," she said, and pulled her dark ponytail across her mouth to hide her smile.

Karen sat down, massaged her feet, and picked out thorns. "This was the brainiest idea you could have had. I've never run any course so slowly or so painfully. And don't you dare tell Enrico about this. He'd laugh me off the team."

Yasmine, still struggling to check her laughter, said, "Maybe there are some differences between us. Run with your shoes on, and I'll run barefoot."

Karen laced up her shoes, her feet still prickling. She watched as Yasmine laid a branch from an olive sapling across the track. "This will be our starting line," she said. "Now, when you run, stop slamming your feet against the ground. Sometimes you press your feet too hard against the earth. You should feel like"—she paused and chewed on the tip of her ponytail—"feel like you're running on a field of eggs and you're going to try as hard as you can not to break any."

Karen stood up, pressing her feet down tenderly. "Eggs?"

"That's right. You don't want to pound the ground, you want to roll over it."

Karen looked skeptically at Yasmine, wondering if this wasn't going to be another barefoot fiasco. Why would Yasmine want to help her? Karen wondered. Why would she want to share her secrets? Yasmine, tall as a pine tree, stood staring at her, waiting to see if Karen would trust her enough to take her advice. She was probably wondering why Karen wasn't training with Tami and Shira.

Karen suddenly smiled. She had nothing to lose, and neither did Yasmine. They had already crossed one line just by being alone together. Why not try another? "O.K., coach," she said, moving behind the starting line. "I'll try not to make too many omelets."

On their next lap, Karen resisted the urge to throw her feet into the ground. Eggs, she kept saying to herself, and though she had a hard time admitting it, it seemed to work. She landed gently midfoot, increasing her speed toward the end.

"Better," said Yasmine as Karen leapt over the branch. "Would you like to do some more?"

"Would I? Of course! I could run here with you all day."

Karen let Yasmine lead her through a few more drills. Finally the sun started to sink behind the mountain, and they had to stop. Lying under the shade of a tree, Karen offered Yasmine the last sip of water from her bottle. Yasmine, Karen noticed, didn't talk a lot. She seemed content to listen to the birds and the wind.

"That was the best workout I've had in ages. Thank you, Yasmine. I think that if we keep training together I'll sail across that finish line way ahead of Rana and Tami."

Yasmine eyed her critically. "Is winning all you care about?"

Karen bristled at the harshness of her tone. "No, it's not all I care about," she said, "but it's a big part of it."

Karen looked away. Yasmine could never understand the other part, the part that had to do with her dad.

Running was all he had ever wanted to do. Now that he couldn't run, she would do it for him. An awkward silence fell between them.

"I hope I didn't get you in trouble with the lunchbox," said Karen.

Yasmine rubbed her arm and screwed up her face. "My brother Abdullah was pretty angry. He suspected *you* of switching the boxes." She giggled. "I couldn't tell him that I was the one who did it. But I'm not sorry. It was the only way I could think of getting us together. Somehow I knew you'd understand." She smiled at Karen. "Do you know what Abdullah calls you?"

Karen shook her head, feeling a strange queasiness in her stomach. "What?"

"The girl with the eyes." Yasmine laughed, and then sighed. "Too bad I couldn't get that new lunchbox you bought. With five older brothers and sisters, I've never had something new—always scratched and torn hand-me-downs." She picked a thorn from her worn lavender skirt.

The girl with the eyes, thought Karen. It's he who has the scary eyes. "Why does your brother call me that?"

"Because you're always staring at us."

Karen felt her face flush. "That's not true. I don't stare. He's always staring at me."

Yasmine stretched out her legs beside Karen's. They were darker, thinner, and longer. She rolled her ankles and flexed her toes. "Don't be mad. I always stare at you, too." She smiled shyly. "That's how I found out that you were like me. Most of your friends don't even see us. All they see are Arabs, and they wouldn't be able to tell one of us from the other. Except you. You seem to study us, as if through a microscope. The same way I look at all of you."

Karen squirmed. Yasmine was right—she always found herself examining them and wondering what it was like to be them.

"What do you see when you look at us?" asked Karen.

"Same thing you see," said Yasmine. "That's what's so confusing. We seem almost the same, except for a bit more color here or a lighter shade there, and yet there's this barrier between us."

"No man's land?" said Karen.

Yasmine laughed. "I guess you could call it that, but it isn't as pretty." She pushed herself up and stretched. "I have to go now. It's getting late."

"Me, too. Will you come back here to run tomorrow?"

Yasmine smiled. "Of course. You still have a long way to go until you'll be as good as I am. But don't worry, with my help you'll breeze across the finish line first."

Karen flinched. Yasmine didn't seem to notice. She turned, and Karen watched as she disappeared around the bend to somewhere on the other side, where there was another hole in the fence.

CHAPTER 10
JOE

"Well, look who's here! Red as a tomato and dripping like one, too."

Karen jumped. She had just crawled through the hole back into the avocado grove when she bumped into Joe.

"Oh, hi, Joe. What are you doing here at this hour?"

"I was just about to ask you the same question." He picked a leaf from one of the trees and turned it over, showing her a bunch of whitish dots. "I wish these buggers knew what time it is. See these little holes? If I don't catch the pests infecting these trees, we won't have many avocados." He picked off a snail and squeezed it between his thumb and forefinger. The crunch made Karen cringe.

"That's disgusting. And to waste an evening chasing after those things."

Wiping off his hand he said, "At least when I'm on the run, I'm out to catch something. What are you running from, Karen?"

Karen shrugged. She tried not to stare at Joe's empty sleeve. She often felt shy and hopeless with Joe, as if his missing arm were somehow her fault. Instead she looked at his mop of sandy brown hair, his mud-caked pants and rubber boots. He reminded her of one of his trees.

Joe laughed. "You don't have to answer that. I remember your dad was just the same. I'd find him out here before sunrise looking just as you do now. Red and sweaty, but with a cherub-like calm on his face. As if he had stepped out of this crazy world for a moment to catch his breath and couldn't understand how he was suddenly back on earth."

Karen smiled. Joe wasn't afraid to talk about her dad, and she could listen to his stories for hours. "You mean Dad also used to run out here on his own?"

"Not only in the grove, Karen. He had a special track. He never told me where, said it was his secret, but I had a pretty good hunch."

Joe glanced over his shoulder into no man's land, and suddenly Karen had a pretty good idea, as well.

"Come on, you're looking wilted. You need a drink," Joe said.

He picked another leaf on their way to the water main. Turning on a hose, Karen held it over her head. The water splashed over her, cool and refreshing. "Here, Joe, feel this." Holding out his hand, Joe let Karen pour cool water over it, too. She shut off the hose.

"I noticed a hole in the fence," said Joe. "Seems it's gotten bigger in the last little while."

Karen squeezed out the water from her hair, avoiding his eyes. "You're not planning on fixing it, are you?" she said, trying to sound as if she couldn't care less. "I mean, why should you bother? It isn't like anybody goes in or out or anything. Who would be crazy enough to go into no man's land? You know, there are ghosts there that probably wouldn't want to be bothered."

Joe nodded. "Still those same ghosts? They must be over a thousand years old by now." He sat down under an avocado tree, resting his back against the trunk. His legs, too long for his body, sprawled out in front of him as if he were a lazy daddy-longlegs. He reached deep into his pant pocket and pulled out an orange.

"You look like you could use some vitamin C. Have a seat."

Karen sat down opposite Joe. She wondered how he would peel the orange. Though she wanted to offer to help, she didn't want to embarrass him. Holding the unpeeled orange to his mouth, Joe took a deep bite out of the skin, spitting the navel aside.

"Smell that citrus. Doesn't it just make your mouth water?" He smacked his lips noisily. Sliding his thumb under the rind, he gradually peeled off the thick orange skin with his hand. The glands in the back of her mouth contracted.

"Pretty good, aren't I?"

"You make it look so easy." She watched him tear a section off with his teeth.

"You want your own?"

"Sure."

Resting his half-peeled orange on his leg, he dug into his other pocket and pulled out a second orange. He tossed it to Karen, who caught it with both hands.

"You try it," he said, "if it looks so easy."

Karen slipped her left arm behind her back. The orange fit just like a softball into the palm of her hand. She rolled it around until the navel was facing up and took a deep bite.

She thought her cheeks would cave in. The explosion of bitter-tasting rind made her face scrunch up, and her tastebuds constricted from the sour spray. Joe watched her seriously, but a faint smile played on his lips.

"Good?" he asked.

"A bit bitter," said Karen. She slid her thumb under the peel, forgetting that she had nicked it on a thorn earlier. A stinging pain made her yelp as the citric acid touched the open cut. She tried pushing the orange peel back, but as the juice spurted out and dribbled down her arm, her fingers became slippery, and the orange flew right out of her hand and rolled in the dirt.

"Damn!"

"Don't curse. You're not doing badly for your first time," he said.

"I'm not done yet," said Karen.

She picked up the hacked-at orange, the exposed parts black from the mud. She slipped her thumb under the peel again, this time less deep. She knew she wouldn't be able to take the peel off in one smooth cut, so she picked it off by bits. Attracted by the sweetness, flies buzzed by her head and settled on her sticky legs. Once she reached out with her left hand and smacked them away, but when she saw Joe's face, she brushed them off with her free leg instead.

"There," she said, holding up the peeled orange.

"Looks great, but maybe you want some of mine?"

Karen frowned at the battered orange. Where white skin remained, it had turned muddy from the dirt on her hand and the roll on the ground. It was a jagged mess, resembling a dog-eaten tennis ball more than a home-grown navel orange. Disgusted, she tossed it aside.

Joe threw her the other half of his orange. She caught it in one hand.

"Hey, don't look so gloomy. These things take practice, and fortunately for you, this is one loss you don't have to deal with."

Karen spat out a seed. "How do you do it all the time?"

Joe leaned back against the tree. He pulled out a pen knife, and placing a stick between his knees, began to whittle.

"They say that when you lose someone you love, you feel like you've lost a part of yourself. Ever hear that expression?"

"Sure," Karen mumbled. "I've heard it." She popped an orange section in her mouth.

Joe whittled silently for a few moments. "Sometimes, the saying goes, it's like losing a limb." He shrugged. "I just know that when I woke up and found out I'd lost part of me, I wasn't sure I could go on. I never loved my left arm. Never thought about it. Just took the old thing for granted."

Karen shifted uncomfortably. "I guess you learn to live life differently once you've lost something," she said.

He stopped whittling and looked at her. "Funny thing, that word—lost. When I came back, people would whisper, thinking I couldn't hear. 'There's Joe—he lost his arm in the war.' I thought that they were reprimanding me. 'How careless, that Joe, went out to war and just lost his arm. Can't he keep track of anything?'"

Karen giggled in spite of herself. Joe smiled at her and wiped his knife on his pant leg. "Silly of me, wasn't it?" He held up a crude hand he had just whittled. It had five oddly shaped fingers bent in the middle.

"Joe, that's disgusting!" said Karen.

"What if I used some hot-pink nail polish?" He laughed. "Just kidding, but it is great for getting to those hard-to-reach spots." Holding the stick, he scratched his back. "You just don't know what you're missing!"

Karen got up. "I think I'll pass just the same." As Joe hopped up, Karen realized how agile he was, and that strange feeling of hopelessness swelled inside her once more. Life was so unfair sometimes.

"Do you want to come over for dinner? Ben's over as usual. I think Mom really likes him, even though he blushes like a lobster."

Joe tossed his back-scratcher onto the ground. "A lobster? Can't say I've ever had dinner with a lobster. He won't make dinner of me instead, I hope."

"Don't worry, I'll protect you. Mom says that she's never seen a better lobster trap than my mouth."

Joe wrapped his arm around Karen's shoulder and gave her a squeeze. "I've heard that your mouth should be listed as a deadly weapon."

Karen stuck out her tongue but didn't shake off his arm. As they neared home, she grew nervous.

"Joe? You won't tell Mom where I've been, right? She doesn't like me running on my own."

Joe shook his head. "Well now, Karen, I wouldn't be one to go telling tales on anybody. Besides, I know that you can't tie a runner down. I think it was your dad who told me that runners don't believe in boundaries or borders. 'Finish lines are for crossing,' he'd say, 'not for stopping at.'

Ever see a runner stop dead in his tracks after crossing the line? No, he just keeps on going."

Karen remembered watching her father soar past the finish line and keep on running, until, like a wind-up toy that wound down, he would finally slow down and then stop.

"So you wouldn't tell even if you thought someone was crawling through the fence and running outside of the avocado grove? Let's say in no man's land?" asked Karen. She kicked a pebble out of her way, not risking a glance at Joe.

Joe shook his head again. "Never met a fence I liked," he said. "If anyone asks, I won't lie. 'There's been some action going on around the hole in the fence,' I'd say. 'I've heard talk that the spirits have been woken up again.'"

"Ghosts?" said Karen, and they both laughed. Then Karen did something she hadn't done with anyone since her father had been gone. She snuggled close to Joe, just like she had always done with her dad. Karen felt him stiffen, then relax. He smiled down at her.

"Must be ghosts," he said. He bulged out his eyes to look possessed and whispered, "We shouldn't disturb those ancient spirits, or evil things might happen. But don't worry, I'll let you know if it is ever really unsafe to run there."

Karen hugged him closer. Her secret was secure, but even though she laughed along with him, she wasn't so sure that there weren't some spirits living there. She only hoped they would protect her if she ever needed it.

CHAPTER 11
CLEANING CRAZE

"Your boyfriend's looking at you," Tami whispered in Karen's ear.

Karen felt her face flush. "What are you talking about?"

Tami snickered. "As if you don't know. That Arab kid at the back of the bus stares at you all the time."

Karen didn't have to turn around to know who Tami meant. She had felt Abdullah's eyes on her. Karen and Yasmine had been meeting secretly every other day for the past week, ever since Karen's barefoot run. But the day before, Yasmine confessed that she thought Abdullah was getting suspicious, and that they would have to be more careful.

"I don't know who or what you're talking about," said Karen. "I think you need your head examined!"

Tami made little kissing noises and tossed another handful of popcorn into her mouth. "Then how come you're so red?"

"Because I'm choking on a burnt popcorn kernel," said Karen, coughing.

Tami laughed. "Nice try, but everybody's talking about it. I think he likes you."

"Don't be stupid, Tami. He doesn't even know me, and I've never said two words to him. Your imagination is working overtime."

Tami popped another handful of popcorn into her mouth without offering any more to Karen. "I don't know, Karen," she said slowly. "I'm not one to make up stories, but some of the other girls were asking me where you've been this week, and why you never train with any of us on the days we don't have practice. Shira said that maybe you've found a better partner because we aren't good enough for you. A barefoot partner maybe?"

Karen swallowed hard. A silence had settled as the kids sitting around them listened in. Tami and her big mouth, thought Karen angrily. Why couldn't she just mind her own business?

"Don't be ridiculous, Tami. You know how over-protective my mother is these days. She won't even let me near the door without a detailed itinerary of where I'm going and with whom."

Karen heard the kids behind her fall back into conversation. Tami nodded and shrugged. She didn't look convinced, even if it was an excuse they all understood. Karen shifted nervously in her seat. Was he really staring at her again? She smoothed down her hair and wound it into a ponytail. She didn't dare turn around. Tami was probably exaggerating. Imagining things that weren't there.

It was the *chamsin* that was making everyone crazy, thought Karen. If the dry, hot wind didn't break soon, they'd all bite each other's heads off. Her mother had been especially short-tempered lately, but Karen was used to it. She would get that way every year as July drew near.

Karen sighed and looked out the window. She could hear David at the front of the bus arguing with Ellah. He sounded upset, just as he had the night before when she'd found him ripping the month of July off his calendar and tearing it into shreds.

"What are you doing, David?" she had asked him.

"How come," he said to her, "when you're alive, everyone celebrates the day you were born, but when you aren't here anymore, they only celebrate the day you died? It's stupid!" He threw the shreds of paper onto the floor.

Karen shrugged. "I don't know, David. I never really thought about it."

"And you know what I hate most of all?" he asked, rubbing at the tears that had gathered in his eyes. "In July Mom won't even bake her chocolate cake, because Dad said the sticky icing was his favorite." He scowled at Karen, as if somehow she were partly to blame for doing away with their dad's birthday. "From now on, I'm not going to any more deathdays, only birthdays!" he said, and stomped out of the room to barricade himself behind the couch.

Karen had picked up the pieces of paper and hidden them in the trash, wishing she knew how to clear up the confusion in David's mind. Their dad's birthday, being so close to the day he died, just made it all that much harder to accept. Every year they seemed to be preparing for his surprise party, only the surprise was always on them, because he never showed up.

"Did you hear that Enrico has almost settled the contract for a new place for the track?" asked Tami, poking Karen in the ribs to get her attention.

"Where?"

"I don't know. The deal isn't closed yet, so everything is still hush-hush. But my dad said that Enrico is thrilled about it. He's been trying for years to find a permanent place for us to train. And if it works out, then the first time around our new track may be the race!"

Karen laughed. "How exciting! Well, they won't be able to keep it a secret for long."

"I'll see you tomorrow," Tami said, and smiled. She climbed over Karen and grabbed her bag from the luggage rack, pushing her way off the bus.

Karen, still deep in thought, got off last. As the bus drove away, she saw Yasmine looking at her out the window, but then her face disappeared and the dark, angry glare of Abdullah was reflected in the pane.

Karen quickly turned away, but not fast enough to stop the goose bumps on her arms.

That night she woke up from a nightmare in which Abdullah spied on her from behind trees with his piercing scowl, as if he blamed her for something she hadn't done. It wasn't as if she had anything to be ashamed of. But his eyes kept following her. Even Tami had noticed him watching her, she thought with a shiver.

The next day Karen pushed off the bus first. She had to hurry. It was Friday, and her mother would be waiting for her to clean her room and help make dinner. Fortunately, on Saturday she'd be free to run.

"Karen? Is that you?" her mom called as the door slammed behind her.

"Who else could it be, Mom?"

Mrs. Silver poked her head out from the kitchen. She was dressed in her sweats and had her hair tied up on her head. This was her Friday afternoon cleaning attire.

"Come here for a moment, I need to talk to you. Are you all right?"

Sliding into the seat opposite her mom, and dumping her schoolbag, Karen got ready for the lecture about how her room was a total disaster area and would soon be sealed up by the government toxic-waste department for emitting noxious chemicals.

"I'm fine. I said I'd clean my room today."

"Yes, that's a good idea, but not what I wanted to talk about." Her mother shifted awkwardly in her seat and cleared her throat. "You know—wait, do you want to drink something?" she asked, rising from her chair.

"No thanks."

Mrs. Silver sat down again and rearranged the strands of hair that had come loose. "You know"—she paused and polished the corner of the table with her sleeve—"that next month will be the fourth year since—"

Karen pushed away from the table, scratching the chair legs on the floor.

"Karen, sit still. I'm talking to you."

Karen pursed her lips together. "I know what you're going to say and I don't want to talk about it."

"Now, Karen."

Karen took a deep breath. After keeping quiet for so long, she thought it would be hard, but the words tumbled out faster than she could stop them.

"I don't want to talk about it. I don't want to keep remembering every year. I want to forget."

She leaned across the table so her face was two inches from her mother's. "I don't need to talk about it, think about it, and bring it up every year. It's over. Finished. Like a lost race that you can't run again. Nothing can change the results." She backed away, feeling suddenly cold, and rubbed her arms. "Can I go now?"

Karen watched as the color drained from her mother's face. She still wiped the same spot on the kitchen table. In a low, quivering voice she said, "It's about time you started to deal with"—she stumbled over the words—"with it." She looked pleadingly at Karen.

"With it?" Karen repeated. "You can't even say what *it* is. What do you mean? That Dad left one day and never came back? That we never said good-bye? That he was fighting a war he didn't want to fight and died in a strange country? I don't need a ceremony every year. I just want to go on where we left off. I've got a race to train for. I have to concentrate on that." She picked up the chair and placed it neatly beside the table, all the while squeezing back the tears stinging her eyes. "Dad would have understood. Even David understands. So leave me alone, because I don't want to talk about it ever!"

"I'm just trying to make this work, Karen. Stop making it so hard for us." Mrs. Silver held Karen by the arm. "Things change. Families change." She sighed. "And I wish you would be more accepting of Ben. I know he'll never be your father, but Ben is someone I care about and I think you need to give him a chance. We have to learn to be a family again and do things together."

Karen shook her arm loose. She blinked back her tears. "I'll try, but there's one thing you should never forget,

Mom. Even though I run on a team, we runners run to be alone. Don't push me to try and be someone I'm not."

She walked upstairs and closed the door to her room. Picking up her smelly T-shirt, she crammed it into the laundry basket. She shook out her bedsheets, wiped her desk till it shone, and stacked her schoolbooks into a pile. When she was done, she flopped onto her bed and stared at the ceiling.

Downstairs she heard her mother vacuuming and dragging the furniture from one side of the room to the other. It was as if she were trying to put things in order, trying to find the missing pieces and make their lives tidy again, like they used to be before Karen's dad had died.

Karen let her tears flow, grateful that her sobs would be drowned out by the drone of the vacuum cleaner.

CHAPTER 12
BITTER ALMONDS

Karen woke up with a start. She had gone to sleep in her jeans and school shirt. Rolling out of bed, she remembered it was Saturday. Yesterday's fight with her mother still weighed heavily on her mind.

David's silly giggles reached her ears, along with another voice that she thought she recognized and rather wished she hadn't. As she threw on a clean T-shirt and a pair of shorts, she listened to the noises downstairs. They reminded her of the Saturday mornings when her dad was alive.

Dad used to wake up early, his footsteps pounding down the stairs like aftershocks from an earthquake. He'd putter in the kitchen, whistling some old song while the smell of perking coffee seeped into Karen's dreams, carrying her away to foreign lands. Then Mom would tiptoe downstairs and drink her coffee on the porch so as not to wake her and David. They would talk and laugh in whispers while Dad did his morning stretches before his run.

Karen would drift back to sleep to those sounds. Like lullabies, they lured her into believing that they would always be there. The Saturday-morning conspiracy, when Mom and Dad would talk about all the things they would do in the future—when Karen was out of school for the summer, or when David was old enough to walk, or when they had enough money to take a trip.

Then one day those special Saturday mornings stopped. Dad's footsteps disappeared with Karen's dreams, and Saturdays became just a quiet day of the week when she didn't have to get up early for school.

Holding the end of her shoelace, Karen paused before tying the last bow. She listened again. It was Ben's voice, and he was telling David a joke. Her brother's high-pitched giggle infuriated her. How could he laugh like that, especially on Saturday! Was she the only one of them who was still loyal to the memory of her father?

"Well, you sound like you're having a good time," said Karen as she walked into the kitchen. No one had heard her come down the stairs. They looked surprised to see her, as if they had forgotten about her, she thought.

"Karen, why don't you come and join us for breakfast? I was just going to put on a pot of coffee for Ben. You'll have a cup, won't you, Ben?"

Ben smiled. "I'd love to, Barbie, if it's no trouble."

Mrs. Silver looked at Karen. "It's no trouble at all. We would love to have you stay."

Karen knew that "we" was meant to include her. She filled up her water bottle. Yesterday's fight had passed like a flash storm.

"Go ahead, you guys," Karen said, avoiding her mother's eyes. "I'm going out for a run. I've got to be in shape, since there's only two weeks left before the race."

Karen heard her mother stifle a sigh. "Karen, maybe you could skip today. Come join us instead. It would be nice for us to go out all together for a change, like a family. Ben brought David a glass container to make an ant farm in, and we thought we'd go out hunting for ant hills this morning."

David perked up. "Ben's an *ant*emologist. He spends his whole day just watching ants."

Ben wiped some maple syrup off his hand. "That's an *ent*omologist, David, and it's only a hobby. I also study other kinds of insects. I'll show you a few of them today. So, what do you say, Karen?"

"Won't you join us, honey?" asked her mother.

Mrs. Silver wanted to call a truce. Karen watched David sprinkling Ben's French toast with sugar and was surprised at how natural it was for him to hang out with Ben, like trading in an old pair of running shoes.

"Every day is crucial, Mom. I can't afford to miss any training time."

Ben must have seen the hesitation on Karen's face. Before she could go on, he said, "Leave it, Barbie. If Karen wants to run before breakfast, let her go. Maybe one day she'll show me some of her running tips. I could use a little more exercise these days." He patted his belly. "And it is a beautiful day to be outside. Have a good time, Karen. I hope we have a chance to sit and talk some other time. I'd like to hear about your training. Barbie tells me that you're quite a runner, just like Michael was."

Karen almost choked to hear his name mentioned. "Yes, my dad was something special," she said, feeling a rising lump in her throat. "I've got to go now before it gets too hot." She grabbed an apple from the table and let the door slam behind her.

The air was hot and dry. Although it was still early, Karen could feel the *chamsin* rolling in. One of the few Arab words Karen used, she liked to say *"chamsin"* for the way it rolled off her tongue and sounded so much like the hot desert wind that dried the sweat on her skin before the drops could even form.

She would need to drink a lot today and stay under the shade of the branches as much as possible. She reached the avocado grove and ran straight for the hole in the fence, slipping through easily.

Karen looked for Yasmine, and when she didn't see her, she decided to start with an easy warmup. After a few arm swings and some skipping, she tried running backward until she collided with a tree. Already she felt her muscles beginning to loosen up.

Starting slowly, she followed their route. Like the beginning of a new friendship, Karen tried to anticipate the turns of the track before she rounded each bend. The spicy zatar plant filled the air as her feet crushed the brown spiky twigs beneath her feet. She easily rounded the slope by the almond tree. As she reached the crest overlooking the Arab village, she raised her arms to brush the pistachio tree, whose crooked branches bent over like a camel's hump. The grasses and trees were a hundred different shades of green. Karen knew that in a few weeks everything would turn brown. Spring was never long enough. Because it hardly ever rained past April, by July the earth was too dry to keep the flowers blossoming.

She absorbed the fragrances and the colors. Her feet, becoming familiar with the track, were learning the lay of the land. She heard the birds in the distance, and the wind through the leaves followed her with a friendly rustle and buzz. Morning air, thought Karen, had a special quality about it. It was fresh, untouched, and ready for what the day would bring. Later it would turn even hotter, a real scorcher. She could tell by the way the hot air seemed to want to squelch the cool air into the ground. Even the flies would be late coming out, too lazy to fight the heat.

She knew that she didn't have long to run before it would be unbearable. Dehydration and sunstroke could creep up on her before she even knew it. As she increased her speed, she spotted a lithe figure looking like a shadowy sprite weaving through the trees. Yasmine came running toward her, her face flushed and her breath coming in uneven spurts.

"Sorry I'm late." She paused to catch her breath. "Abdullah wouldn't let me out of his sight. It took me forever to sneak away from him."

Karen fell into step beside her. "Are you sure he didn't follow you?" She glanced over her shoulder, half expecting to see him hiding in the shadows.

"Pretty sure, but don't worry about Abdullah—he's harmless. Let's not waste any more time. I'm ready to run."

After a short walk they broke into a run, then walked again until they had cooled down. Finally, sweaty and tired, Karen sprawled out under an almond tree, making room for Yasmine, who first scooped up a handful of almonds from underneath it.

"Aren't those too bitter for you?" asked Karen.

"Abdullah likes the bitter ones. I'll give them to him, and maybe he won't ask me any questions."

"He would like the bitter ones," said Karen, rolling back to sit on her haunches, and looking out at the sun-baked field.

"He's not all that bad," said Yasmine, stuffing the almonds into her pocket. "He's just a bit overprotective. Abdullah's only a year older than me, but he thinks that being fifteen makes him the boss."

Karen shrugged. "I'm glad I don't have a big brother bossing me around." She looked up at the sun. "It's almost lunchtime. Mom will be really annoyed if I'm not home on time. I wish you could come over for lunch."

Yasmine laughed and sat up. "I would love to see my father's face at that suggestion. As it is I've stayed too long and they are probably wondering where I've disappeared to."

Karen smiled, thinking that Abdullah's angry scowl would look like one of the evil ghosts who haunted no man's land. She hopped up, but as she leaned down to pull up Yasmine, her giggles caught in her throat.

There he was, facing her, his eyes the color of thunderclouds. "Yasmine!" he shouted.

The rest of the sentence Karen didn't understand. At the sound of Abdullah's voice, Yasmine disappeared like a frightened field mouse into the underbrush, leaving Karen to face him alone.

"Stop shouting at her like that," said Karen.

Abdullah, with his legs spread and his arms locked firmly across his chest, jutted out his chin and pulled himself up as tall as he could in order to look down on Karen, who stood only a few feet away.

"Mind your own business," he said. "Stop interfering."

That was the first time he had ever spoken to her. Though the words were said softly, the tone was threatening. Karen didn't flinch.

The sun beat down on her bare head. The flies had finally come out, landing on her sweaty arms as if waiting to see what would happen. Even the leaves on the trees that had been lazily riding the breeze seemed to stop and listen.

"We *were* minding our own business," she answered, "until you came charging over here. Yasmine was on her way home. So why don't you just get going? She'll follow in a minute, if *you* can stop interfering."

Karen kept her own voice low and calm like Abdullah's. She watched as Yasmine stepped out cautiously from behind the trees and moved toward her brother. Karen stayed put. She wasn't sure if it was fear or stubbornness that kept her fixed to the spot. Her legs felt like two ancient tree trunks rooted to the ground. Leaning slightly forward, she rested her hands on her hips, drawing herself up as she faced his silent challenge.

"You had better go now," said Abdullah, still not moving, waiting for Karen to back down. "And stay away from Yasmine."

"Why should I? We're friends." Karen waved to Yasmine, and ignoring Abdullah, called out to her, "Yasmine, I'll be back here this afternoon when it's cooler. I'll meet you then."

Yasmine nodded.

Karen turned her back on Abdullah, and swinging her arms as if she wasn't the least bit afraid, as if her heart wasn't pumping wildly, and as if her knees weren't threatening to collapse beneath her, she walked toward her side of the fence.

"Yasmine will not come today," Abdullah called as Karen reached the hole. "Not tomorrow, or ever again. And you," he shouted, raising his voice above the chirping of the birds and above the rustling of the trees, "had better keep off our land!"

Like the blast of a plane slamming through the sound barrier, Abdullah's words reverberated inside Karen. "Your land?" she repeated, feeling her muscles tense. Her back was still to him, but she knew he had heard her.

"This is *our* land," said Abdullah, his voice deep and steady, "and *you* are trespassing."

Karen straightened her shoulders and rested one hand on the fence. She knew she should just crawl through to the other side and go home, but she couldn't make herself move. She inhaled until her lungs strained against her chest and her breath screamed for release.

Abdullah's voice grew stronger, just in case Karen hadn't heard, in case his words had missed their target. "This is our land," he said again, "and always has been. Nothing you do or say will ever change that."

Karen turned around and shielded her eyes from the sun's piercing glare. "No, Abdullah," she said. "This is our land. We fought for it. We won it. You've decided that it belongs to you because you claim to have been here a few years before us and have buried a few ancestors here. We've buried a lot more people than you for this land, even if their bodies are not planted here."

They stood transfixed. Yasmine had moved to stand beside Abdullah. Karen, alone, stood at the fence, but felt that safety was miles away. She recognized her own seething anger reflected in Abdullah's dark, unyielding eyes.

"We have let the land run wild," she said, "so as not to antagonize your people, but one day we'll grow crops here." Karen snapped off a twig from a nearby branch. "This is our land. So *you* had better get off and quit trespassing on *my* racetrack."

Karen couldn't hear Abdullah's answer. Her pulse, throbbing in her ears, was deafening. Then she saw Yasmine hang her head, and instantly she regretted every word. She hadn't meant to say that. She didn't want to fight about land. She really didn't care whose land it was. But that's what Arabs and Jews fought about. It was their only common language.

"Yasmine," Karen pleaded as Abdullah grabbed his sister's arm and pulled her back toward their village. "I'm sorry, I didn't mean it. Please say you'll meet me here this afternoon."

Abdullah tugged at her wrist and Yasmine didn't look back. The two figures, united against her, disappeared among the pine trees.

Karen kicked the fence. Everything had gone wrong. She didn't want to fight with Yasmine. It was Abdullah's fault—he had provoked her! She stamped her foot on the ground, feeling the fury rage inside her.

"Abdullah," she said aloud, knowing he could not hear her, "you may be the most infuriating person I have ever met. But I won't let you get the better of me!"

CHAPTER 14
TOO FAR TO TURN BACK

"You're late, so we started without you," Mrs. Silver said as Karen walked into the house. "And you're all red. Wash your face before coming to the table."

Karen touched her cheeks, feeling the anger still burning like red-hot coals. She splashed water on her face, hoping it would also cool her temper.

As Karen slid into her seat, she noticed that Ben was sitting in her father's place at the table. His face was flushed, and there was an edge in his usually even tone.

"Ben, could you please pass the salad to Karen?"

Ben shoved the salad bowl at Karen. "You're wrong, Barbie," he said.

"I am not wrong," Mrs. Silver answered curtly. "I refuse to play by terrorist tactics. If they want the land, let's discuss it. Soil needs water, not blood, to be fertile."

Karen caught David's eye. He shrugged. "They've been arguing the whole day," he whispered. "Ben found a nest of army ants, and I managed to collect a queen and a few workers. Do you want to see them now?"

"Maybe after lunch, David." Karen pushed the sprouts to one side of her plate and hid them under the lettuce. She wanted quiet but knew that these arguments about what piece of land belonged to whom went on forever.

"How much land do we have to live on?" asked Ben, slamming his fork on the table. "Don't you think that if we had any to spare we'd share it? If we don't hang on to what we have, they'll push us into the sea. They conquered the land from the Turks, and now we've conquered it from them and have come to settle it. That's the way life works. You take what you can get. I don't see the Americans giving back land to the Indians." He scraped his chair away from the table. "Why can't the Arabs get land from their own kind, instead of trying to take the little we have?"

Mrs. Silver, clutching the salad bowl, began heaping food onto Karen's plate. "Mom, I already have salad. I'll never finish all that."

Mrs. Silver ignored her and continued to dump out lettuce and tomatoes until she had practically emptied the bowl. Karen dove to catch the cherry tomatoes that were rolling like cannonballs across the table.

"So it's better to fight until our husbands, fathers, and sons have died?" said Karen's mom, her voice rising. "To fight for a piece of land until there is no one left to populate it? Is that your solution? Well, it isn't mine. We have to compromise, don't you see?"

Ben rubbed his eyes and heaved a sigh. "Barbie, I believe in compromise, too. But it takes both sides to reach

an understanding, and they're just as stubborn as we are."
He shook his head. "We've been fighting for so long we
don't know how to talk anymore."

Karen listened to them drone on. She had always tuned
out when her parents argued, saying she didn't care. Now
she felt her insides shrink. Her mother was right—fighting
over land was stupid. Karen feared that she had lost
Yasmine's friendship because of it. What had made her react
as she had with Abdullah? Just the thought of him infuriated
her all over again, and her head started pounding.

Karen covered her ears with her hands. "Stop! Stop it,
please! I just don't want to hear any more."

Her mother looked up, surprised. "We have been going
on a bit too much." She stared at her untouched plate. "I'm
sorry, Karen. I didn't mean to upset you. It's this whole
business with no man's land that got us going. But you're
right, let's not argue while we eat. Discussion over."

"Good," said David. "Now can I show Karen my ants?"

Karen almost choked on a slice of cucumber. "What
about no man's land?" she asked.

"I don't think we should talk about this anymore at
the table. It will give us all indigestion. And no ants at the
table, David. Karen will see them later."

"Please tell me," said Karen, trying to hide the anxiety
in her voice.

"Your running coach has been trying all year to
convince us and our Arab neighbors from the village
to turn no man's land into a racecourse. He says he's tired
of being pushed from one place to another all the time. He
says that it's time his athletic organization be taken

seriously." Karen's mom popped an olive into her mouth. "He expects me to get involved, because of you and your father's love of the sport."

"Who would think that weed-infested dump could cause such problems?" said Ben.

"Michael loved that weed-infested dump, Ben. Like Enrico, he had great plans for the place. He donated money to the sports council for his dream of one day turning no man's land into a racecourse. Michael was someone who never stopped trying to make his dreams come true."

Karen barely noticed the moment of strained silence. "Did Enrico get the land?" she asked. "Will the race be held there?"

Her mother shrugged. "You know how things work in this part of the world, honey. Can you pass the bread to Ben?" She smiled at Karen. "Nothing gets decided until the last second. But yes, there's a very good chance that we'll all come around in the end."

"So, Karen, think you'll be ready for the race?" asked Ben, smothering his bread with butter.

Karen stuffed a tomato in her mouth and nodded. "I'm trying to get into shape for it," she said. She couldn't believe it: no man's land turned into an official racecourse. Not in her wildest dreams did she ever imagine something like that could happen, that both her community and Yasmine's would actually agree on something. She couldn't wait to tell Yasmine. It would be different now. They wouldn't have to hide. They could run together on the field, side by side.

"Great. I'm sure you'll do well," said Ben, unaware that she had stopped listening.

Mrs. Silver smiled and shook her head. "Karen? You're dreaming." She tapped Karen's arm, and smiled apologetically at Ben. "Her father tried to make her a runner, but I think she lives more in the clouds than with her feet on the ground."

Ben laughed. "I don't know about that, Barbie. She's built herself the body and, I think, even the mind of a runner. Don't arch those eyebrows at me, Karen," he said. "Just because I don't run myself doesn't mean I don't know anything about it. Runners are stubborn, independent, and like to be alone."

Karen's mom whistled. "You certainly have her pegged. I've never met a more stubborn individual."

Ben rolled his eyes and winked at Karen before she could answer. "Really?" he said. "I think I have."

It was obvious he meant her mother. Karen thought she would throw the lemon meringue pie in his face, but instead her mother smiled and blushed. "Well, I know when to compromise and admit that my adversary is right."

David groaned. "Can I go yet?"

"Finish your juice."

"Mom, I'm going to shower and then go back out for a late afternoon run," said Karen.

"All right, but make sure you're back well before dark," said Mrs. Silver. "You've other things to do today besides running. What about that history test?" She stacked the dishes, balancing the cups on top. "Put these in the kitchen, will you? Ben and I have some work to do, so we'll be in my office if you need anything."

Karen dumped the dishes in the sink. Work to do. She doubted that.

"I'll be at Ellah's," said David and gulped the juice. "I've almost perfected a new wrestling hold and am going to try it out on her."

"I don't know what to do with that boy," their mother said, shaking her head.

Karen took advantage of her mother and Ben's discussion of David and slipped upstairs before they could ask her to help wash the dishes. She showered and sat down on her bed to study history, but her book read like a continuation of the argument downstairs and of her run-in with Abdullah. She forced herself to reread the pages for the test, but her thoughts kept wandering back to their discussion at the table, and she knew what her father would have said. "Land cannot belong to anyone. It is only lent to us to use while we are on this earth. We are all renters, none of us are owners of the world."

Karen slammed her book shut. There was no escaping the circle of history.

When the sun finally started its westward path over the Lebanese hills, Karen left the house. She hoped Yasmine would meet her. She couldn't wait to tell her the great news about no man's land.

Karen ran past the community club house, down the path by the old stone house that Joe had turned into a gardening shed, and out into the avocado grove. By the time she reached the hole in the fence she was panting. The sun threw long shadows on the ground. The birds had drifted off, getting ready for evening, and a sacred hush had fallen over the grove.

Karen waited for Yasmine by the almond tree, hoping that their argument wouldn't really stop her from coming.

To pass the time she ran on the spot, struggled through push-ups, and eased into some stretches. Running was a loner's sport, Ben had said. Karen loved the time alone, although she had also come to enjoy running side by side with Yasmine. If Yasmine didn't show, she didn't know what she would do.

As the sun sank lower, Karen realized that Yasmine wasn't coming. Soon it would be dark and too late to run. Her mother would be worried if she came back after sundown, that is if she wasn't too wrapped up with Ben.

Karen started off at a slow pace, still hoping Yasmine might appear. For the first time running alone made her uneasy. She wondered if it was the twilight shadows, or the early evening noises she wasn't used to.

As she reached the peak overlooking Yasmine's village, the farthest point from the avocado grove, Karen thought she heard an unfamiliar cry. She sensed the rustle of feet in the underbrush and quickened her pace. Glancing over her shoulder, she caught sight of one of the boys from Yasmine's village. A feeling of panic swelled in her chest. She stumbled over a root but got herself back on track.

"Go, Karen! Run back!" Yasmine's voice came rushing at her through the trees like a sharp blast of thunder, followed by peals of laughter. Karen stopped and turned.

"Yasmine? Where are you?"

There was no answer.

A current of fear went searing through her body, sending warning signals to each nerve ending. The danger was so near she could smell it and hear it in the deafening beating of her heart.

Then all at once she saw them.

There must have been at least five, six, or even seven agile boys swinging their arms and calling out to her. From somewhere inside she sensed her only chance to survive was to run. She turned and fled, the boys chasing closely behind. She had started the uphill climb away from Yasmine's side of the field. It was too far to turn back.

As she ran, her brain tried to make sense of it all. Had Abdullah come back with reinforcements for revenge? To claim the land? Was he going to show her that he could take what he thought was rightfully his? History all over again. Abdullah had declared war and had set out to ambush her.

The boys' voices, ringing out strange and foreign, bombarded her from every side. She knew from the sounds of their feet that they were gaining on her.

The sky had grown dark. The underbrush snagged at her feet, and the fear of what they would do if they caught her confused and slowed her down.

Again she heard a pitiful cry. This time she wasn't sure if it was her own voice, or Yasmine's.

The shouts and crashing of feet against the earth grew louder, until all the field echoed with their sounds. Karen tried to block them out of her mind. Ignoring the thorns that stung her legs, she fought to keep the fear in her throat from trapping her breath.

Concentrate, she said to herself. She visualized the course in her head. She forced her feet to feel light and airy, as if she were running on eggs. But with each egg she landed on, Karen imagined her friendship with Yasmine shattered into thousands of broken shells beneath her, destroying every chance that things could have been different.

Karen ran on. Tears stung her eyes, blurring her vision.

She could hear the boys behind her stumbling, unused to the tricky turns and upturned roots. She knew the path blindfolded and trusted her instincts. They started to fall behind, though still their calls reached her. She knew she was close to her side now. Would they dare follow her through the fence? Would she be safe on the other side? Don't think, she told herself. Just run.

As Karen saw the fence come into sight her pace quickened as if she were reaching a finish line. Only this time there would be no flag waving. No prizes or gold medals. Her heart beat wildly, and her side throbbed each time she inhaled. She was almost home free. Then on the last step, she stumbled.

She hadn't seen the overgrown root. Soaring above the ground, her hands flailing sideways, she landed just inches from the fence.

Everything went black.

CHAPTER 15
WAR GAMES

Karen groaned.

The muffled sound rose from deep within her, and she lifted her head. A throbbing in her temple sent a surge of pain coursing through her body. Resting her head on her arms she licked her lips and recognized the salty taste of her own blood. Her lip must have split from the fall. She dug her elbows into the rocky ground, shifted onto her knees, and crawled forward.

The sky had grown dark, and she shivered, wondering how much time had passed. The outline of the hole in the fence teased her with the promise of safety. She didn't know exactly why it mattered so much, but she was sure that she didn't want to be found in no man's land. She had to reach the other side, and then think about what to do next.

Gathering all her strength, she dragged herself forward. The spiky thorns scratched her bare arms. Finally, reaching the hole, she pulled herself through.

Like a soldier in enemy territory, Karen edged on, creeping on her stomach, her face close to the dirt. The huge branches of the avocado trees swayed in the wind, casting sinister shadows. Even the crickets' song sounded strange and threatening, as if they were conspiring against her in a language she didn't understand.

Tears and sweat stained her cheeks. "I have to get a hold of myself," she whispered. "Mom's probably worried sick." A sense of urgency swelled inside her and pushed her on. There could be enemies lurking between the trees, waiting to surprise her.

She made it to the next tree. Thinking of her mother brought back visions of her father. He had taught her not to be afraid, saying the rockets always sailed above them and the gunfire was too far away. He promised her that they would always be safe.

He had been wrong.

"You lied," Karen accused him, as if he could hear her. Leaning back against a sturdy tree, she stared at the night sky. "You wanted us to feel that we were untouchable, but we aren't. Now the truth hurts more than the fear would have hurt then." The truth hurt even more than the pounding pain in her head.

"If you had taught us to be afraid of them, I wouldn't have even tried," said Karen, looking up at the stars. "I would have known that we can never trust them." Inside, disappointment stung with a faint but ever-persistent doubt that her friendship with Yasmine was ruined forever.

In the stillness of the night, with only a few stars in the sky, Karen listened, trying to remember what happened, but all she could recall were the sounds. Yasmine's cry came back, ringing in her ears. How had Yasmine known the boys would come after her? Karen drew her knees to her chest and hugged them tightly. A chill in the night air made her shiver. She should have known that once their secret was out, there would be trouble.

Pulling herself up, Karen took a deep breath. "You can make this last lap home," she told herself, wiping the tears from her cheeks. "Mom's waiting for you. Prove to Abdullah and all of them that you can't be beaten so easily."

Dodging from tree to tree, staying close to the trunks for fear that she might be spotted, she left the avocado grove. Half running, half walking, she soon saw the outline of her house in the distance.

Through the screen door Karen could see her mother pacing nervously, stopping frequently to peer into the darkness. Suddenly Karen felt exhausted. She tried to call out, but her voice caught in her throat.

"Karen!" Mrs. Silver cried, running out to meet her. "Where have you been? I was worried sick about you!" She threw her arms around her. "I was going crazy," she said. "I sent Ben to look for you in the grove, and when he couldn't find you, I didn't know what to think." Wrapping Karen in a tight embrace, she hugged her with all her strength.

"I didn't know what to think," Mrs. Silver repeated, and paused as they reached the porch. Looking closely at Karen, she frowned. "Is that blood on your forehead?" she asked, reaching up to wipe away the dark smudge with her sleeve. "And your lip is split!"

Karen shrugged. "It's just a scratch, Mom," she mumbled. "Can we go inside? I'm so tired."

Mrs. Silver nodded. "In a moment. Let me hug you a little bit more. I was so scared, Karen. But you've come home." She held her tightly, and Karen let her body go limp in her mother's embrace.

Later, tucked safely in her own bed, Karen listened to her mother and Ben arguing. Though part of her was there with them in the room, another part seemed to be floating somewhere far away. Her head hurt. A dull, aching pain in her right temple was a constant reminder of what she wanted to forget.

"Keep your voice down, Barbie. Getting excited won't help anything."

"You expect me to stay calm?" came her mother's reply. "I'm ready to scream! I have been through this all before, and damned if I'm going to go through it again. If only I had been there. I couldn't be there for Michael, but this, this I could have stopped. She's my only daughter, Ben!"

"Barbie, be reasonable. You're jumping to conclusions."

Karen's head hurt so much, she wished they'd stop arguing. What good did it do? Just made things worse.

"Mom, I don't think Karen likes it when you yell."

It was David. Sweet David. Karen sighed as a hush settled on the room. She could sleep now.

Sleep for a long time.

CHAPTER 16
JUMPING COLONEL LOOSENS

Moonlight streamed in through the window. The tingle of David's sleepy breath on Karen's face awoke her, banishing her bad dreams.

"Are you awake yet, Karen?" David whispered.

"I'm awake now. What are you doing up in the middle of the night? Mom will have a fit if she finds you." Karen rolled onto her side, wincing from the pain in her head.

David stifled a yawn. "I'm here to protect you. This is my guard-duty shift, and no one is going to get past me. No one is going to hurt you ever again." He stood up, checked the lock on the window, and pressed his ear to the door.

"Don't be silly, David." Karen yawned. "Go to sleep. I'll be fine."

David shook his head. "Oh no. If I had been there in the first place to protect you from Colonel Loosens, nothing would have happened to you. It's all my fault." He came back and stood beside her bed. "Dad would have wanted me to guard you."

Even in the dim light, Karen could see David's eyes were moist with tears. He was trying to stay brave, but his voice shook ever so slightly. She reached out and punched him on the shoulder.

"I couldn't feel safer, soldier, with you guarding me, but it wasn't your fault. I never take you when I go running, if I can help it. Now tell me, who is Colonel Loosens? What are you talking about?"

David, looking grave, bent down to whisper in her ear. "I heard Mom and Ben talking about jumping Colonel Loosens when he comes back to get you. Ben kept saying that Mom shouldn't jump him." David grinned. "That's probably because Mom's a girl, but I'm ready for him. I'm not chicken. I'll protect you now."

Karen laughed. "David, Mom could out-jump Ben any day of the week, even if she is a girl. I think Ben must have told Mom not to jump to conclusions, not 'jump Colonel Loosens.'"

David looked puzzled and a little hurt. "That's what I said."

"It means," explained Karen, "that she shouldn't accuse anyone until she knows what really happened."

David relaxed his post and perched on the end of her bed. "So if Colonel Loosens didn't do this to you, who did?"

Karen shifted uncomfortably. That was a question she needed to answer for herself. "I'm too tired to talk now. I want to go back to sleep."

David sucked his lower lip into a pout. He was about to argue when they both heard footsteps shuffling toward the door. David jumped to attention and grabbed his rifle.

"It's Colonel Loosens!" he whispered.

Slowly the doorknob turned. The hinges squeaked reluctantly, and a shadowy figure hovered in the doorway.

"Take one step farther, and you're dead meat!" said David. "No one gets past me. I'm a crack shot!"

"David Silver, what do you think you're doing up at this hour!"

Karen flicked on the bedside light, and before them in her bathrobe and fuzzy slippers stood their mother. David's mouth fell open.

"I thought I heard noises in here," said Mrs. Silver. "Is he bothering you, Karen?"

"It's all right, Mom. David was guarding me in case I needed anything during the night, but I'm feeling better now."

"Are you? Good. Get some more rest and we'll talk in the morning. Come on, David, I'll take over guard duty from here."

Karen closed her eyes. Their hushed whispers receded into the night, and she waited for the quiet, but instead she heard her father's voice in her dream saying, "It's the after-moment that kills something inside of you." If Karen could have, she would have rewound the last day and done it differently. But it was too late. Karen pulled the blankets tighter around her, wondering if Abdullah was also awake, feeling his own after-moment, and if it hurt him as much as it hurt her.

"Hi, how are you feeling?" asked her mother. The morning sun flooded Karen's room with light.

"Better." Karen smiled.

"I'm glad to hear it." She gave Karen a peck on the cheek. "It looks like you've only suffered a few scratches, outside of that ugly bump on your forehead. I don't think you should do any strenuous activity for the next while though."

No strenuous activity. Karen recognized the determined look on her mother's face. Even with a bump on her head, Karen knew what she meant.

"I'll be fine for the race, Mom," she said.

Her mother forced a laugh and gave her an awkward hug. "Don't you think it's premature to talk about that? There will be other races, honey." She sat down on the edge of Karen's bed.

Karen felt her breath come faster, and she struggled to stay calm. She looked her mother straight in the eye. "I'm better now," she said. She stretched her arms above her head. "I should get up or I'll miss the school bus."

Mrs. Silver smoothed Karen's hair from her forehead. "Let's not rush into things. I've decided to give you and David a day off from school. You've had a bad"—she hesitated—"fall and need time to recuperate." She smoothed Karen's pillow and tucked in the sheet. "It might take awhile."

"Mom, you've got to let me run." Karen felt herself growing desperate. Her voice rose and cracked. "It's my first real competition. I promised Dad that I'd run as soon as I was old enough. There are only twelve days left! I have to qualify in this race, or Enrico won't let me compete in the 10K in Spain."

"Spain?" Mrs. Silver laughed. "You're always in a hurry to get somewhere. You're growing up too fast, but I guess I'd better start getting used to it." She traced the creases of Karen's blanket and gave her a kiss on the forehead.

"I'm O.K.," Karen said. She looked up desperately at Ben, who had tiptoed into the room. "Ben, you tell her. I'm going to run in the race. I can do it! I have to." She struggled for control, to hide how much everything ached. The pain inside would be unbearable if she couldn't run the race.

"Your mom isn't saying anything of the sort, are you, Barbie? Just rest for a bit now."

Karen forced herself to smile at Ben. He sounded as if he was on her side, despite the worried frown he tried to hide.

David came stomping into her room. "Karen's up again!" he yelled.

"Shh, David, not so loud. Your sister must have one doozer of a headache."

"Wow! Look at the size of that thing," shouted David, pointing at her bump. "So now can you tell me how it happened, Karen?" he asked. "And don't leave out any of the details—I promised Ellah I'd tell her all about it."

Karen closed her eyes and wished she could close her ears and block out David's overexcited yapping. Now was the moment she had been dreading. She realized that her mom hadn't asked her. Did she know? Did they all suspect? Had they all jumped to the right conclusion?

Karen knew that if she told the truth, any chance of friendship with Yasmine would be gone. Instead of a fence with a hole, there would be a wall with guards. Their paradise racecourse would remain a neglected no man's land.

But could she let Abdullah get away with it? Abdullah's eyes watching her, mocking her, Abdullah hating her. Well, now she hated him more than ever. She wanted him to suffer for her suffering. Because of you, she screamed inside, I may not be able to run the race and Enrico may never give me a second chance. Yes, Karen thought, Abdullah deserved to be punished for what he had done. She just had to say the word and no man's land would stay sealed up forever. She sat up. What choice did she have?

Then Karen heard a different voice. "Is winning all you care about?" Yasmine had asked her. She shifted uneasily on her bed.

"Well, Karie," said her mother as she picked up Karen's hand and held it warmly in hers. "Tell us what happened. It will make you feel better."

Karen swallowed hard. She felt her mother staring at her, waiting for her answer. They all knew. But they were waiting to hear it from her.

Waiting for her to throw the first stone back.

Karen wished her father were there. He'd know what to do. And that's when she noticed Ben. He was looking at her, waiting to hear what she had to say, not what he wanted to hear.

"If you aren't ready to talk about it, don't," he said, moving behind her mother and resting his hands on her shoulders. "I don't think we should press her, Barbie. Give her time to clear her thoughts. Come on, everyone, I've made a Lucky Ben's breakfast, and it's waiting downstairs."

David swiveled around. "What's the 'lucky' for?"

Ben laughed. "You'll be lucky if you get any before it's all gone. My breakfasts are so good they're world-famous. You guys didn't know that I am also an amateur chef!"

David got up, torn between his stomach and Karen's story.

"Go ahead, David. My story isn't so exciting. I think I just got caught in the crossfire of some game."

"Crossfire? Whose game? What game?" asked her mother.

Karen shook her head. "It was dark and I couldn't see." That was true, she hadn't seen exactly who it was, though she had no doubt.

"But you must have heard something," Mrs. Silver pressed her.

Yes, thought Karen, I heard. She remembered the sounds of kids running and calling to each other. She looked at her arms. No bruises, no cuts. The scratches were from the thorns. Only the bump on her head, but maybe that was her own fault? She had been careless and in her panic had tripped.

"I heard some kids playing around. And when I saw it getting dark, I hurried and must have stumbled on my way back."

Barbie reluctantly got up, letting go of Karen's hand. "I don't know who you're protecting, but when you're ready, Karen, let me know. I'll take care of it. I've got friends in the government."

"But I told you, Mom. It was just an accident. Why, what do *you* think happened?"

Red blotches appeared on her mother's cheeks. "I just thought, well, never mind. I'll go have some of Ben's breakfast. You'll join us, won't you, honey?"

"In a minute, Mom." Karen watched them leave the room. Her mother, resting her arm on Ben's, suddenly looked so fragile, as if life had become too heavy for her to carry by herself.

• • •

The day passed slower than an uphill run. Every time her mother peeked in, Karen shut her eyes, feigning sleep. She needed all her strength to stand up to her mother, yet she wasn't sure she had it in her.

Later in the afternoon, Karen heard a loud knock on the door, and before she could answer, Tami burst in. "Karen, you're alive!" she cried.

Karen sat up and brushed her hair over her forehead to cover the ugly bruise. "Of course I'm alive, what did you think?"

Tami tossed her schoolbag on the floor and sat down on the edge of the bed. Her face was flushed, and Karen realized enviously that she had been at track practice. Her shirt was still damp and beads of sweat streaked her face.

"So, you're O.K.?"

Before Karen could answer, Tami babbled on. "You should have seen me at track today. I was incredible! My best time ever. It was so great. Enrico just couldn't stop going on about me. We'll be meeting every day after school, even if it's just to stretch. Enrico wants to keep us in top shape until the race." Tami clapped her hands. "I'm going to take this race without a doubt, especially now that you won't be running!" She paused and giggled. "Oops, sorry, I didn't mean to say that."

Karen clenched her teeth. "Who says I won't be running, Tami?"

Tami rolled her eyes. "Come off it, Karen. We all heard about what happened to you. They say that you'll never run again. You've been traumatized for life."

Karen snorted and kicked Tami from under the covers. "Enough dramatics, please. You're making me ill."

Tami giggled and rolled off the bed. "Those are dark chocolates, aren't they? My absolute favorites," she said, licking her lips at the sight of a box of candy Karen's mother had bought.

"Yes," said Karen. "Eat as many as you want. I can't have any."

Tami grabbed a handful. She popped two in her mouth. "Delicious! You don't know what you're missing. Why can't you eat any, are you allergic?"

"No," said Karen, throwing off the covers and finally feeling that she wanted to get out of bed. She swung her feet over the edge and stretched. "I have to watch my weight. I wouldn't want any extra pounds slowing me down during the race."

Tami clamped her mouth shut. Her cheeks, still swollen with chocolate squares, flushed even redder. Grabbing her schoolbag, she stuffed the other chocolates into her pocket. She pulled out a crumpled envelope from her bag and tossed it on the bed.

"Here, Karen," she said, wiping her mouth with the back of her hand. "Your Arab buddy made me bring this to you."

Karen blushed. She could easily read Tami's expression. "Thanks," she said. "I'm sure it was a pain to bring it."

Tami shrugged. "Anything for a friend in need." She turned to leave and stopped at the door. "Karen, I don't think you have a chance of qualifying in this race, especially after what happened." She paused and smiled. "But I respect you for trying, and I love a good challenge."

"Don't worry, I'll give you one," said Karen. "Thanks for coming, Tami. I'll see you at practice tomorrow—and the rest of the week."

Tami shrugged and swept out the door.

Karen waited until she had clomped down the stairs. She checked the seal of the envelope, wondering if Tami had been tempted to peek inside. Even though it was crumpled, it looked unopened.

Karen held it in her hand, unable to break the seal. It was probably a letter of apology from Yasmine. Karen wasn't sure she was ready to read it. Sitting down by the mirror, she stared at her reflection. A greenish blue bump rose from her forehead. Her hair was a mess. Slowly she began brushing through the knots and tangles.

Karen heard her mother answer the front door. By the sound of his voice, she knew it was Joe. She picked up Yasmine's envelope again—she'd open it later.

"Hi. Am I disturbing you?" Joe asked as he knocked on her open door. He was still in his work clothes, and in his hand was a bouquet of wildflowers.

"They're beautiful!" said Karen. "Come in, I'll find a vase."

Joe lay the bouquet on Karen's desk and moved Yasmine's envelope aside. "How are you feeling today?"

"Fine," said Karen. While she was arranging the flowers in a vase, she glanced up to see Joe staring at the envelope with a puzzled look on his face. "Ignore that," she said. "I haven't opened it, yet." Karen could tell by his expression that he had noticed the strained letters, not written by someone familiar with Hebrew lettering.

"Don't you want to open it?" he asked, handing it back to her.

"Later," said Karen, taking the envelope and putting it on her night table. "It's not the right time now."

"It's never the right time," said Joe. He laughed. "That's what I used to say to your dad. He'd always be trying to get me to run with him, and I'd say, 'It's not the right time, Mike. It looks like it might rain,' or some other lame excuse." Joe shook his head and stared at the floor.

"Then there was the business with no man's land," he went on, his voice so low Karen could barely hear him. "Your dad worked so hard to get everyone to agree to share it, but the only thing they all agreed on was that it wasn't the right time to make a decision." Joe bit his lip and turned away so that Karen couldn't see his face. He walked to the window, looking out at the hills that reached to Lebanon and beyond.

"All those missed times, Karen. We should have had more time with him, and now it's too late. I miss your dad. We were like brothers, you know."

He looked so lonely, his gangly limbs framed in the afternoon light, like a lost child. Karen went and stood beside him.

Joe laid his hand on her shoulder. "You're going to run the race, aren't you?" he asked. "It would have meant a lot to Mike."

Karen smiled. "I'll be there, even if it means my mom chasing me around every bend in the track." After a moment she frowned. "I only hope she'll let me go to Spain."

"Don't worry about your mom, Karen. She'll come around. You just get yourself across the finish line."

Karen threw back her shoulders and straightened her spine. "I'll get there, Joe. You'll see."

Joe gave her a hug. "Take care of yourself," he said and slipped out of the room. Karen reached for the envelope from Yasmine and tore open the seal. A delicate bracelet made of colored threads was tucked inside. Yasmine had carefully woven together bright, bold colors—sunflower yellow, deep orange, magenta red—and framed them around a turquoise braid.

"How beautiful!" said Karen's mother, peering over Karen's shoulder. "Such a fine weave. It must have taken hours to make."

Karen frowned at her. "I didn't hear you knock," she grumbled.

"Sorry. The door was open, I didn't think you'd mind. Isn't that so sweet of Tami? You should wear it only for special occasions, otherwise the threads might fray."

Karen thought about telling her mother who had really made the bracelet. Who had taken the time to weave together all those colors. Who had cared enough about her to make something so beautiful. But that would have been too complicated. She took the bracelet from her mother and tied it around her wrist.

"No, Mom," she said, thinking of her dad. "I think now is exactly the right time to wear it."

CHAPTER 18
MAKING AMENDS

"You are not going out alone, and that is my last word on the subject!"

Karen's mother stood with her back to the door. The whole day at school Karen had been dreading this moment, wondering how to tackle the biggest obstacle in getting back to the grove to run. With the race only one week away, she felt too jumpy to hang around the house watching David collect ants. She also hoped that she might see Yasmine, though Karen wasn't sure she had the courage to go back into no man's land.

"I need fresh air," said Karen.

"I'll take you for a walk," said her mother.

Karen rolled her eyes. "Put me on a leash, it'll be easier for you to make me heel."

Karen heard laughter from the kitchen. Ben came out holding a cup of coffee and handed it to Karen's mother. "May I interrupt?" he asked.

Mrs. Silver frowned. "It depends. Whose side are you on?"

Ben smiled. "I'd rather not answer that. I just wanted to point out that Karen wouldn't be completely alone if she were to go to the grove now. I saw Joe on his way there earlier. It seems like there's a lot of work going on in the area."

"Well, what about it, Mom?"

Her mother didn't look very happy but seemed unable to find a good enough reason to object. She took a sip of coffee. "Just don't stay too long."

"I won't. Thanks, Mom!" Karen gave her mother a peck on the cheek. "Bye, Ben, and thanks."

She sped through the kibbutz and into the avocado grove, to the reassuring cover of the big trees. She wanted to hear the silence again and smell the earth. She wanted to feel the wind wrap gently around her and remember that she had good memories here as well as the ones from the other night.

As she neared the border to no man's land, she paused, wondering if she was ready to go back inside. She missed their track. Even more, she missed Yasmine. Since the night that the boys had chased her, Karen had passed by Yasmine on the bus, but a shyness seemed to make them both awkward. Even Abdullah, Karen noticed, avoided looking at her. She hoped Yasmine had seen her wearing the bracelet.

Suddenly she stopped short by the hole in the fence, wondering if her imagination wasn't playing tricks on her. The strange voices, the shouts—they were there again!

"Joe!" Karen shouted as she ran through the grove looking for him.

Joe, hunched over an avocado sapling, looked up in surprise. "Hey, Karen, I was hoping you'd come."

She grabbed his arm. "The boys! I can hear them in no man's land."

"Easy, Karen, it's the only arm I've got." He stood up and brushed the dirt from his knees. "Relax. I'll go with you and we can see how far they've come." He led the way through the grove back to the hole in the fence.

"Over there!" said Karen. "They've almost reached the grove." A whole gang of kids from the village was running through no man's land, their voices raised, sounding almost triumphant.

"What are they doing? Have they come to steal the land right out from under us?"

Joe laughed. "I thought you knew. They've begun to clear the land."

Karen backed away from him. Her thoughts were all confused. Who had given them the land? She didn't want to know. "I'm getting as far away from here as I can!" she shouted.

She turned and ran. Feeling the earth fly beneath her feet, feeling the wind rip wildly through her hair, she reached the edge of the grove panting and sobbing. Her heart beat loudly and her temple throbbed. Pausing to catch her breath, she clutched her head in her hands, trying to steady her trembling body. But she couldn't run from them forever. She had to go back and see for herself what was going on.

Karen turned around and, at a snail's pace, headed back for no man's land. Reaching the hole in the fence, she sat down beside a tall tree. The kids from the village and some of her neighbors were busy clearing the area, dragging rakes along the trail and snipping off low-hanging branches. No one noticed her. Suddenly Karen understood. They were cleaning the track for the race. Enrico had finally been given the land to build a racecourse. It all made sense.

As she spied on their slow progress, she was suddenly distracted by the rattle of the barbed-wire fence. She looked up, half expecting to see a frightened animal trying to escape the commotion. Instead she saw a dark-haired boy who was working hard to pull up the fence and roll it aside.

The barbed wire that rimmed no man's land was rusty and resisted being coiled into an iron ball of scrap. Karen watched as the boy struggled with it, carefully trying not to scrape himself or get snagged by sharp pieces of wire. He was inches away before he noticed her. He dropped the fence abruptly, and a deep flush spread across his face. Stumbling backward, his legs became tangled in the loose strings of wire. In a last-ditch effort to save himself from falling, he grabbed onto the low-hanging branch of a pistachio tree.

"Abdullah," said Karen. She spoke his name softly, feeling a rush of emotion surge through her as the syllables tumbled off her tongue.

He looked nervously over his shoulder, hoping, Karen assumed, for someone to come over. For the strength his buddies gave him.

"It's just you and me," she said, standing up and moving toward him.

He didn't answer, fumbling impatiently with the fence instead. Each desperate tug at the rusty wire only made matters worse. The fence seemed to be playing a nasty game of cat-and-mouse with him, but Abdullah remained undaunted.

Karen could feel her breath coming faster. "You're good at tearing things down and destroying things," she said, shifting her eyes from the fence to his face. "Yasmine and I could have been friends, but you ruined it all." Her hands trembled, and tears of anger stung her eyes. She blinked them away.

Abdullah tried to free his feet from the tangled wire but snagged his shirt instead. He cleared his throat. "It's not what you think," he said.

Karen dug her fingers into her arms to keep from shaking. "What do you mean? I was there, wasn't I? I heard you. You and your buddies chased me through the field and I've got this lump on my head to prove it." She brushed her hair away from the discolored bruise on her temple and saw him wince.

He shook loose from the fence but didn't run. Instead he stepped closer to her. Shoving his hands into his pockets, he tried to look fearless, but his eyes, dark and wide, darted nervously. "It's not what you think," he said again. "Let me explain."

Karen took a deep breath and exhaled slowly. "There's nothing to explain, except perhaps to tell me what I did to make you hate me so much. At least now we're even on that score. I can hate as easily as you can."

Abdullah didn't move. He just stood watching her, glancing back for a moment at the freedom of the field behind him. "You've got it all wrong. It was a mistake."

"What was the mistake—letting me go and not finishing me off?" Karen heard the hysteria rise inside her, and her voice cracked. She backed away from him. "I want you to know that even though you're Yasmine's brother, I'll never forgive you! Now, go away. I never want to see you again!" She gulped in air, waiting for him to turn and leave.

Abdullah's shoulders hunched forward, and the corners of his mouth twitched. "Why won't you give me a chance to explain?" he said. She heard a strange quiver in his voice. "Your people are always like that—jumping to conclusions, not willing to listen."

Karen turned her back to him but didn't leave. Her mother had been quick to jump to conclusions, and now Abdullah was accusing her of the same thing. "All right," she said, brushing impatiently at the tears on her cheeks. She kept her back to him. "I'm listening. This better be good."

Abdullah kicked at the pebbles on the ground. "Could you at least turn around?" he asked. "I feel strange talking to the back of your head."

Karen turned around slowly. Abdullah ran his fingers through his hair and moved back to lean against a pistachio tree.

"It is all my fault." He tripped over the words, adding, "But not how you think. I knew Yasmine would go back to meet you. My father would have been furious with me if he knew Yasmine was running again, and with one of you."

He blushed again. "She always gets off easy, and I'm the one he blames when she does things he doesn't approve of. As if she ever listens to me." He stopped, searching for a sign of sympathy, but seeing none, turned to examine a pebble by his foot.

"Yasmine and I argued, and I guess someone overheard us. Later, when my friends saw Yasmine trying to sneak away, they decided to follow her. By the time I arrived, the chase was on. Yasmine tried to warn you, but everything blew up out of control. I ran after my friends to try and call them back. It was just a big game for them." Abdullah paused. "They wouldn't have hurt you."

He had thrown out the words so quickly that he was nearly breathless when he stopped for air. He dug his hands deeper into his pockets and kicked at the coil of wire. "Yasmine and I sneaked back later, but you were already gone."

Karen swallowed hard. "It's easy to come up with excuses now. How do I know you're telling the truth?"

Abdullah bit his lip and shrugged. "You won't, I guess. But it's my word. Honest. I knew it would be dangerous for the two of you to meet here, but I thought Yasmine was the one who had to be protected."

They stood staring at each other as the seconds ticked by, and Karen saw something in him that she had never seen before. His eyes, still dark and guarded, had a strange flicker in them. He seemed to be waiting for a sign from her.

"Abdullah!" someone in the field called.

Abdullah swung around, glancing furtively back at her.

He shifted his weight awkwardly, wanting to turn and run, but waiting to be sure she understood.

"Your friends are calling you," said Karen.

"I know. I had better go. We're getting the land ready for the race."

Karen smiled, noticing that he hadn't said whose land. She shook her head. "I don't understand. I thought it would take another hundred years for both of our communities to agree to share the land."

Abdullah shrugged. "Yasmine told my father what had happened to you in the field. He was really angry at us for going behind his back. Then that one-armed guy came with Enrico to talk to him about using the land for a track, and he got the other villagers to agree. Maybe he was worried about what your people would do if we didn't agree to share the land, maybe he felt bad, or maybe he even thought it was a good idea."

"Abdullah!" the boys called again.

Almost reluctantly, Abdullah turned toward where his friends were working. "Will you run in the race?" he asked.

Karen shrugged. "Why? Do you care?"

"Yasmine says you're good." He picked up a pebble and tossed it in the air.

"I am good," said Karen. "I outran all of you guys, didn't I?"

Abdullah looked up. He didn't flinch, didn't turn away, but this time she didn't see the hate in his eyes.

"Enrico says I'm the fastest runner on the boys' team."

Karen folded her arms across her chest and shook her head. She didn't know what to make of Yasmine's brother, talking to her now as if nothing had happened between them.

"If I win our race," Abdullah continued, "my father will believe that I have talent, and I might be able to convince him that Yasmine does, too. He may let Yasmine back on your team, as long as I am around to watch her."

Then Karen understood. It was his way of saying he was sorry, of saying that maybe it wasn't so bad if she and Yasmine stayed friends.

"Abdullah, *yulla,*" the boys called.

"They're yelling for you to come," she said.

Abdullah smiled at her. It was a shy, slight upturning of his lips, and then it disappeared. Karen watched him run back to his friends, knowing that something had changed between them.

CHAPTER 19
THE FINISH LINE

"Hurry, Karen! You're going to be late!" David yelled from outside the house.

Karen took one last look in the mirror and adjusted the bill of her father's lucky cap to shade her eyes. With a little adjustment in the back, it sat just right.

"O.K., Karen," she told herself. "Today's the day!"

Skipping down the stairs two at a time, she hurried to catch up to her mom, David, Ben, and Joe on their way to no man's land, now the new racecourse. They wanted to cheer her on across the finish line.

"That's Michael's hat!" said Mrs. Silver. "Wherever did you dig up that old thing?" She smiled at Karen. "Your dad never ran a race without it. He would have been thrilled to see you running today, and wearing his lucky cap."

Karen thought her heart would jump out of her chest it was beating so hard. "I'm ready now, so let's not waste time. I can't wait to get to the track."

Taking the road that ran from their kibbutz to the Arab village, Karen led them to the new racecourse. "It would be faster through the grove," she told her mom and Ben, "but you must see it from the right angle." Just before reaching the Arab village, they stopped.

"Here it is!" Karen exclaimed.

No man's land, once a field of overgrown weeds, thistle, bushes, and rocks, was now neatly cleared, framed by the kibbutz grove on one side and the village's fallow sheep-grazing land on the other. Scattered picnic tables gave the impression that it was a quaint nature reserve.

Ben whistled. "Wow! Who would have thought we'd live to see Michael's dream come true?"

Mrs. Silver smiled and leaned over to give Karen a hug. "I'll be proud to see you running here today. You go and do the best you can. We'll be cheering for you."

"Thanks, Mom," Karen said. She turned and ran up to the group of girls from her track team. She had seen the boys' team hovering in the background, waiting for their turn to run.

"Your knees are shaking," Karen told Tami.

"I can't stop them," said Tami. "I'm a bit nervous. Have you seen the legs on those girls?" Tami pointed at a group from a competing team.

Karen moaned. "I've seen giraffes that were shorter." She turned back to Tami. "But it's speed, not height, that matters, right?" She took a deep breath. This was it. The first three to run across that finish line would be on their way to Spain. "All we have to do is run better than everyone else."

Tami groaned. "But it seems that every thirteen-year-old in the whole country has come to compete!"

A plane passed overhead, breaking the sound barrier.

"Can you imagine what it would be like to soar at such speed?" asked Karen. "I've always dreamed of one day flying off to someplace exciting. This is our chance."

Tami rubbed her palms together. "Don't get your hopes up too high. I can feel the tingle of victory," she said, the confidence coming back to her voice. "You girls had better watch out!" She leaned over and squeezed Karen's arm. "I'm glad you're running with us, Karen. Winning wouldn't have been the same without you. Just try not to crowd me."

"Thanks, Tami. I'll be sure to wave when I pass you by."

Tami laughed. "You wish!"

Karen tightened her shoelaces, adjusted her cap, and again tucked in her shirt. Any moment now, Enrico would be over to give them a final pep talk. Karen was surprised to see how many people had come from the Arab village to watch the races. But though she scanned the crowd, the one face she most wanted to see wasn't there. Yasmine hadn't come.

"All right, girls," Enrico shouted above the noise of the crowd. "You must concentrate. Focus. Let's show them all! Take your places!"

Karen squeezed in beside Tami and Rana. Enrico patted her on the shoulder. "Focus, Karen. Remember the drills."

Karen nodded. She wiped her hands on her shorts and took one last look around. She could do it.

"On your marks! Get set! Go!" The gun sounded, echoing the excitement in the air.

Karen took off. She flew out in front of Tami, passed Rana, and kept a safe lead in front of them all. "Focus," she chanted. She refused to let her thoughts wander. "Focus," she said as she made the first turn.

As the hill rose, she knew that soon they would pass the place where once there had been a hole in the fence on her side of the field, only now there would be no hole, no fence. The remains of the fence were jumbled together in a wire ball, thrown to one side of the field like a forgotten relic.

She sprinted forward, keeping her lead. The hill sloped downward, bringing into sight all of Yasmine's village. She pressed on, letting her feet roll over the ground.

Karen swallowed hard. She was coming to the spot where she had first seen the boys and heard Yasmine's cry. The last time she ran this lap, she thought she had been running for her life. She stumbled just thinking about it, and Tami flew out in front of her. Somehow it just didn't feel right without Yasmine running beside her.

"Focus," she said, but her legs had become stiff and held her back. Would they be there again, waiting for her behind the trees, calling her name and chasing her? Tears of anger and frustration stung her eyes. The lead she had was slipping. Rana shot ahead, and a pair of shoes with blue laces was licking at her heels.

She didn't want to give up. She wasn't a quitter. She pushed on, but she had lost the rhythm of her run, and probably would soon lose the race.

Suddenly, from behind the trees, she heard a voice.

"Come on, Karen! Push harder!"

Karen thought she had imagined it, but there on the other side of the track, running between the trees, was Yasmine! She disappeared behind the brush and appeared once again. Her dark brown feet flew lithely over the ground, and she held the hem of her skirt in her hands.

Slipping through the pistachio trees, Yasmine, red-faced and breathing hard, ran up beside her.

"I can't, Yasmine," Karen gasped. "I'm afraid. I keep thinking—"

"Then don't think. Run! Follow me."

Karen fell into Yasmine's rhythm and quickened her pace. Yasmine's skirt billowed in the wind like a parachute ready to be swept up and carried across the finish line. The other girls faded into the background, and it was just the two of them again, running side by side.

"Long strides," coached Yasmine as she ran. "Watch the eggs! Don't batter the earth or you'll break them. You can do it, Karen! Give it all you've got!"

Karen put her feet down lightly, landing on the ball of her foot, springing off her toes. Soon she could not hear Yasmine's voice, but Yasmine's rhythm stayed in her heart. As she caught up to the others, she could see Rana sprinting in the lead with Tami not far behind.

Karen's head pounded and her heart thumped like beating drums. The pair of running shoes with blue laces inched up beside her. She could do it. She had to do it. She was almost there.

"Go!" shouted Yasmine. "Do it for us, Karen. You've got to win it for me." Over the throbbing of her temple and the aching pain in her side, Yasmine's voice urged her on.

She would win it for Yasmine, for her dad, and most of all she would win it for herself, to prove to everyone that she was a runner and that nothing and nobody could stop her.

She sped forward, the adrenaline pumping through her like never before. As she neared the finish line, Karen saw the pair of blue shoelaces coming closer, matching her step for step.

The crowd hollered madly. David, perched on Ben's shoulders, was flapping his arms wildly. And in the foggy distance, way past the finish line, on the other side of the border, she saw her father waving his arms. "Come on, baby," he was calling. "Get those lightning legs going."

"I'm coming, Daddy," she cried. "I'm almost there."

With Yasmine beside her, she flew forward, leaving blue-laces in the shadows.

Karen's foot crossed the line. She had made it.

Victory!

But she didn't stop. She crossed the finish line and kept on running.

CHAPTER 20
THE TASTE OF VICTORY

"Come on, Yasmine, can't you move any faster? I know you can speed through this course quicker than any of us when you want to."

Karen had never known Yasmine to move so slowly. She tapped her foot impatiently. After all the feet that had run the course in the last few days, it was smoother than a Persian carpet. Yet Yasmine, dragging her feet along the track, kicking up more dust than a desert sandstorm, was slowed down by every thorn and thistle.

"I don't belong at a victory lunch," she said. "I didn't really run the race."

Karen wiped the sweat from her forehead and shook her head. "Explain that to the judges who saw you fly across the finish line beside me and then disappear like one of the ghosts from no man's land. 'The spirit in the skirt' everyone called you, until *I* set them straight."

Karen tried mimicking the expression of astonishment on the judges' faces. Yasmine had no number, and no one knew who the strange barefoot girl in the purple skirt was, or why she had disappeared before anyone could ask her.

But Karen and Enrico had known. Even if Yasmine couldn't claim a prize, Enrico insisted that with talent and spirit like hers, Yasmine had to join the team in Spain.

Yasmine snorted. "Until you set everyone straight? You had to open your mouth and almost cause World War III to break out at my house. Luckily, Abdullah's win softened up my father. Hold this," she said, shoving a bowl into Karen's hand. She stopped and crouched to pull another thorn from her foot, stalling for time. "Facing my dad, though, is nothing compared to what's waiting for me over there!"

Karen nudged her forward. "You're making too big a deal out of this. Stop being such a chicken."

She looked over to where Yasmine was pointing. To Karen, it was a pleasant, homey picture. The picnic tables by the side of no man's land were overflowing with food. Ben, the amateur gourmet chef, had prepared every dish ever found in a cookbook.

"Get your fingers out of my Caesar salad!" Karen heard him shout. "Make way for chocolate-covered ants! This is going to be an international feast no one has seen the better of!"

Karen sneaked a glance back at Yasmine, who was twisting the sash of her skirt. She looked so frightened and unsure, not at all like the girl who had defied her family to come to the race and urge Karen across the finish line.

"This smells great." Karen sniffed at the bowl Yasmine had passed to her. The rich spices reminded her of how hungry she was. "You didn't have to bring anything, though. Ben loves cooking."

"My mother insisted. She usually makes very good hummus." Yasmine bit her lip. "There she is!" she whispered, pointing at Tami, who was picking out cherry tomatoes from the salad while Ben's back was turned. "She'll probably hate my mother's cooking. It will be too hot for her."

"Much too hot," said Karen. "Too much lemon juice, and probably not enough garlic." She laughed. "That's just the way Tami is. You'll get used to her."

Tami looked up, glanced in their direction, and went back to fishing for tomatoes.

"She hates me," said Yasmine, taking a few steps backward. "I can't go there, Karen. I'm sorry. I'm not ready for this."

Karen tried to see the scene from Yasmine's perspective. Her mother was pouring orange juice into paper cups. David and Ellah were tying balloons to a cactus plant. Every few seconds another balloon exploded.

"David!" cried Mrs. Silver. "You're driving me nuts! I keep spilling the juice! Go collect more ants or something."

Tami was sitting at one end of the picnic bench folding napkins when she wasn't picking at the food. Rana was at the other side arranging the forks. They were ignoring each other completely. Joe and Enrico, standing by the track, were deep in conversation.

"No one hates you, Yasmine," said Karen. "We all just need some time to get used to each other."

"Used to the idea of running together on a track team, or being friends?"

"Both," said Karen.

Yasmine glanced back across the field. "I could run home in minutes," she said.

Karen nodded. "True, but you seem to be having a bit of a hard time moving forward." She gave Yasmine a gentle shove.

"There they are!" shouted Ben. Holding a cake in one hand and waving with the other, he called to them. "Karen, Yasmine, hurry up. All the food is on the table waiting for you two."

Karen linked her arm through Yasmine's. "Take a deep breath," she said. "Imagine that this is your last lap. I know it feels like straight uphill, but this time *I'll* be running beside *you*."

CHAPTER 21
TAKING ON THE WORLD

"My ears are going to burst!" shouted Karen.

Buckled into her seat, she slapped her hands over her ears and chewed noisily on her gum. The roar of the engines grew even louder as the Iberian aircraft took off.

"I hope it isn't Fahad in the pilot's seat," said Tami. "I feel sick, and we haven't even reached cruising altitude."

Karen giggled. "It *is* kind of like Fahad's bus. You. Me. Yasmine. Rana. Jonathan and Omar and Abdullah. Only we're off to Spain and *not* to school!"

Tami shifted restlessly in her seat. "Even the seating arrangements are like the bus. Uncomfortable and unfair! I don't know why I had to get the aisle seat—I can't see a thing from here. Karen, ask Yasmine to switch with me."

Karen shrugged. Rana, sitting beside Tami, had her forehead pressed to the other window. It wasn't only the aisle seat that was bugging Tami.

"Sorry, Tami," said Yasmine. "We flipped a peseta, I got the window seat, and I'm not moving."

Tami grumbled and slumped back in her seat.

"Even in Spain Tami will find something to complain about," Karen whispered to Yasmine. "So, is that a new skirt?"

Yasmine smiled. "You noticed! Yes, my father bought it for me. Isn't it nice?"

"Beautiful," said Karen. "I'm glad our parents agreed to let us take this trip. Otherwise Enrico wouldn't have much of a track team. When my mom gets stubborn about something, it's easier to crack pistachios with your teeth than change her mind! But she really wanted me to go. She said it was what my dad would have wanted. I'll never understand her."

"I know exactly what you mean!" Yasmine laughed. "My dad is just the same—unpredictable."

Enrico stood up in the aisle and faced them. "All right, you kids, listen up now. The plane ride is about six hours, and then we'll drive through the mountains for another two hours to my house. I'll give you kids the afternoon off, but then tomorrow morning first thing we're on the track. You're new to this, so you'll need a lot of work. I expect you all to be up and ready. Don't forget we've a race to win in a few days. That *is* what we came for."

Enrico started to return to his seat and paused. "I almost forgot!" He dropped a magazine into Tami's lap. "Take a look at that, Tami. You and Rana are going to be famous. A full article on the group focusing on you two in *The Runner's Report*."

"What?" Tami grabbed the magazine and squealed. "Rana, look at us! This is incredible! Pictures and everything."

Rana turned from the window to huddle with Tami over the magazine. "My hair is a mess," she moaned.

"Oh, I don't know," replied Tami, "it gives you a windblown look. Very authentic."

"Do you think so?" asked Rana. "Listen to what they say about us over here," she said, and began reading out loud.

"That will keep the two of them busy for a while," said Yasmine.

"And bragging for days!" Karen replied, peeking over at the magazine, but Tami and Rana were hogging it. "It would have been us, you know," she said, turning back to Yasmine, "if you hadn't disappeared before they could snap our picture. Talk about being in the wrong place at the wrong time." She stretched, but the seat in front was too close and squished her knees.

"You didn't have to come chasing after me," said Yasmine. She turned away from the window and smiled at Karen. "But I am glad you did, or I wouldn't be here. Will you come with me exploring this afternoon once we settle in?"

"Sure, though I still can't believe we're really going to race in Spain. My feet are tingling just at the thought of it. Poor blue-laces never had a chance."

Yasmine laughed. "You could have beaten Tami, too."

"I know, and now I have to worry about beating you!"

Yasmine poked her in the ribs. "Not a chance!"

Karen sat back in her seat and sighed. "I'll worry about that later. Ben gave me some money," she said, lowering her voice. "Maybe the two of us can sneak away and do some shopping."

Yasmine glanced behind her at Abdullah, who was playing a heated game of cards with the other boys from his team. "Abdullah will have a fit if I disappear. He told my father he wouldn't let me out of his sight for a second."

"That just makes it all the more exciting," said Karen, poking Yasmine in the ribs and giggling.

"Don't be too hard on him, Karen. Abdullah was the one who convinced my father to let me go. Sometimes he isn't such a bad brother to have around. He's also a pretty good runner."

Karen turned to look at Rana and Tami, who were still poring over pictures of themselves and analyzing each word in the article as if no one else existed. Peeking over her shoulder, she saw that Abdullah and the other boys were arguing over who should deal the next round. As if sensing Karen's scrutiny, Abdullah looked up.

"I don't know what you two are planning, but forget it!" he said, and tried hard to look stern. "I'm not letting Yasmine out of my sight."

"All we'd have to do is run away," taunted Karen. "You'd never be able to catch us."

Abdullah threw his pillow at her and missed, hitting Tami.

"Watch it!" Tami yelled. "You'll crease the magazine. Really, the two of you are acting like such children." She threw the pillow back, which started an all-out pillow war. Enrico was called in to mediate but couldn't get a word in over the shouts and laughter.

"Truce!" yelled Tami suddenly. "The flight attendant is coming with the food cart."

"So how many are you on the team?" asked the flight attendant as she put a tray down in front of Karen.

"There are seven of us," answered Karen.

The flight attendant nodded her head and smiled, as if it were the most normal thing in the world.

Yes, thought Karen, all together they were seven kids. Where she was from, they couldn't have been a stranger mix, but as far as the world was concerned, they were just a small amateur track team from the Middle East on their way to a competition in Spain.

A small team, but together they were ready to take on the world.